BUON GIORNO
ST BRIGID'S

A note on the author

Geri Valentine was born in Dublin and now lives near Dundalk, Co Louth. *Buon Giorno St Brigid's* is the fourth book in the hugely successful St Brigid series which includes *Bad Habits at St Brigid's*, *New Broom at St Brigid's* and *St Brigid's Bounces Back*.

BUON GIORNO
ST BRIGID'S

GERI VALENTINE

POOLBEG

Published 1995 by
Poolbeg Press Ltd,
123 Baldoyle Industrial Estate,
Dublin 13, Ireland

© Geri Valentine 1995

The moral right of the author has been asserted.

A catalogue record for this book is available from the British Library.

ISBN 1 85371 521 2

Cover illustration by Marie Louise Fitzpatrick
Cover design by Poolbeg Group Services Ltd
Set by Poolbeg Group Services Ltd in Stone
Printed by Cox & Wyman Ltd, Reading, Berks.

To Michele with love and thanks

Contents

1

Crosswords with the Contessa

"It's a challenge, that is why I'm going to do it!" announced Aileen firmly, her fair hair glinting in the sunlight, which filtered through the leafy branches of the giant beech tree, known to all as Barney. This tree was the favourite after-school refuge of Aileen and her friends, all third year students at St Brigid's, that famous school on the river Boyne.

"But, Aileen, *ten* crossword puzzles, there is no way you could possibly get so many finished before the twenty-second of the month, we're only coming back from Rome on the twenty-first!"

"I don't care, I'm going to do it," said Aileen stubbornly. "As a matter of fact, I've nearly finished two already."

"The prizes must be good," observed Judith lazily from her branch in the tree.

"It isn't the prize, it's the glory," retorted Aileen haughtily, then relenting she added: "Actually the first prize is a long weekend in the fabulous *Hotel Waterfront* in Galway. I shall give it to Mum and Dad, they'd love it."

1

"You'll never do it," said Josie rashly, "it's much too difficult."

"That's what you said about me making a cake in school once, do you remember, and what happened: I did it and won the bet," retorted Aileen swiftly.

"You two remind me of that story about the Hedgehog and the Fox," said Eithne. "Aileen is the hedgehog and you are the fox."

"What story? I don't remember it," said Josie.

"If you ever paid attention in class, Josie, you'd remember that the hedgehog has only one talent but is really brilliant at that one thing, whereas the fox is clever and smart about many things, but is not brilliant at any one thing."

"And who are you calling not brilliant at anything?" began Josie indignantly, swishing her long ponytail. Then she stopped as they heard someone climbing up the tree towards them.

"Hi chucks, I'm back," a cheerful voice broke the sudden silence. A girl with short crinkly hair framing a mischievous face appeared between the leafy branches.

"Nuala," they all shouted. "It's Nuala!" She pulled herself up on to one of the branches and sat beside Aileen.

"You're early," said Aileen. "We weren't expecting you for ages yet."

"I couldn't bear to be another minute away from school, as you can imagine," said the newcomer, grinning. "The truth is that it suited Mum to leave me back now."

2

"Great," said Judith, "now that you're here, spill the beans about the Celtic Heritage award thing you attended yesterday in Dublin, omitting no detail, however slight!"

"Well," said Nuala, leaning back against the truck of the great beech. "It's hard to know where to begin."

The prize-giving ceremony which Nuala had attended, as winner of first prize in the junior section with her essay "Chanticle of a Chalice" had been a very big affair. Madame Desirée d'Este, newly-appointed special envoy of the European Union, presided and gave out the prizes.

"Go on, Nuala," said Josie, leaning forward in her desire to hear about the prestigious event. "Start at the beginning, you arrived all dolled up with your parents, and what happened then?"

"When we arrived," said Nuala, "we were taken into a very large room with tall windows, where we sat on gilded chairs with blue velvet seats, very swish, facing a kind of raised dais, full of VIPs. The walls had a series of portraits in oils ranged all around them. Someone told me that it had been a State room once."

"What were the paintings like?" asked Judith, who was a keen student of art.

"Don't bother describing them," said Josie, impatiently, "tell us about the special European envoy with the fancy name."

Nuala's face broke into a smile. "They were all pretty horrible, Judith, just painted mug shots of some of the grimmest things in history, except perhaps the Duke of Ormonde, he had a bit of style."

"What was he like then?" asked Aileen.

"He was painted lounging nonchalantly against a table or a desk, wearing his cloak thrown back dramatically, revealing a fine pair of long elegant legs. It crossed my mind several times during the terrible boring speeches we had to sit through that he could have made a fortune modelling tights on TV."

Although this remark was greeted with merry laughter, Josie was still anxious to hear about the special envoy. "What did Madame Desirée look like?" she asked eagerly.

"Oh very very chic in black. Long dress with fancy embroidery, all tiny pearls, I think, around the neckline. Actually, when I went up to get my prize, I noticed she had a matching handbag, sewn with tiny pearls too, it looked brilliant."

"Wow," said Josie obviously impressed. "Was she good looking too?"

"No, not really," was the reply. "She certainly looked very smart though, glossy black hair cut short with two little wings of it curving towards her tanned face on each side. In fact, she looked a tough cookie. The funny thing was I thought there was something familiar about her, though of course I'd never met her before."

"She's been on television a lot lately," said Judith. "You probably saw her without realising who she was."

"Maybe," replied Nuala, "she has a very strong French accent too."

4

"Did she speak to you?" asked Josie eagerly.

"Yes, she spoke to me, just three words: *Trés bien, Mees O'Donnell*," grinned Nuala, speaking in what she fancied was an imitation of the chic Madame d'Este's voice, causing more merry laughter from her friends.

"Did you really get a cheque for a hundred pounds?" asked Eithne, one of the Murray twins, first cousins of Judith.

"I really did but I can't show it to you. Dad took it home with him to cash it for Rome," said Nuala cheerfully. "Sr Gobnait says it's a most expensive place, especially for eating out. Can you believe it, this day week we'll be on our way to the Eternal City!"

"Then it will be *Buon Giorno Roma*," said Aileen. "For them, it will be *Buon Giorno* St Brigid's, of course!"

"It's unbelievable," replied Nuala, "like a dream that can't be happening to us."

"I hope it's not going to be a nightmare," said Eithne, "did you hear that the *Cleaner* is coming with us?"

"You're not serious Eithne," said Josie. "I know she's considered a brilliant English teacher to the top stream but she is awfully old-fashioned and fussy. I only hope we don't see much of her."

"You mean Miss Grimes," said Judith. "I wonder where she got that nickname from."

"We don't know," said Eithne. "Someone took her for one of the school cleaners is one story, but I think maybe it's a play on the name Grimes – you know."

"I wouldn't worry about her, Josie," said Aileen, "she never has much to do with us lower orders."

"Nuala, what do you think of Aileen's latest fad?" asked Josie. "Crossword puzzles! She has entered for a competition to send in ten puzzles by the twenty-second, if you don't mind."

"Poor Aileen," said Nuala shaking her head sadly. "I should have guessed something was wrong when I saw you doing *The Irish Times* one last week."

"Time is running short," said Fidelma, the other Murray twin. "Remember you've only a week left before we go to Rome, Aileen."

Then Nuala, in light-hearted mood, made an offer which she was later to regret many times: "Don't worry, Aileen," she joked. "You can always take them to Rome with you. There's bound to be lots of time between sightseeing and churches and monuments, to do a quick puzzle or two. We'll all help you, won't we?"

"As long as she shares the prizes with us," said Josie.

"We'd look lovely all taking turns at that long weekend in Galway," said Judith. "Of course we'll help, Aileen, bring them along anyway."

"I'll probably have to," replied Aileen cheerfully.

Strange to relate, while the third years were discussing their forthcoming visit to Rome, Madame Desirée d'Este was already in that city. She was in a quiet street, only minutes away from the noise of traffic sweeping continuously across the Via Merulana, waiting impatiently for a pair of massive gates, set in a high wall, to open.

Eventually the gates were opened by a man in uniform, allowing the car to pass through into a circular courtyard, where it drew up and stopped outside the tall narrow house there. It was very peaceful in the courtyard, in sharp contrast to the noise of the city outside the gates. Only the murmur of doves cooing gently in the background and the soft splashing of the fountains playing in the centre of the courtyard broke the warm silence of the afternoon.

Madame d'Este alighted from the car, slamming the door, and went straight into the house where she was met by an elderly woman dressed in black. *"Buon Giorno, Signora,"* the woman smiled, opening the door of the salon for her. "La Contessa is within."

"Grazie, Bella," replied the European special envoy, gracefully sweeping past her in through the open door. The salon which she entered was cool and fragrant with its high ceiling and marble floor. Three tall windows curtained in white muslin, with their shutters half closed against the sun, protected the oil-painted landscapes which lined pale walls. A slight woman, who had been gazing at herself in the mirror above the ornate mantelpiece, swung around.

"Ciao, Desirée," she said. "The usual, I suppose." She busied herself with a decanter and glasses set on a low table beside her.

"What's all this about Roberto having the

negatives stolen from his safe? How could he be so careless!" the newcomer demanded crossly. "I came immediately, as you can see."

The Contessa added ice to the amber liquid in the glass and handed it to Desirée. As the latter took a long drink, the Contessa, unlocking the top drawer of an adjacent bureau lavishly decorated with flowers and leaves, removed some photographs from it. Spreading these in front of her friend, she said: "All the negatives are now destroyed except for these last photographs here."

Desirée picked up one of the photographs in front of her, looking keenly at it. It showed two couples in evening dress, looking very pleased and happy about something.

"That was a good party, I enjoyed it immensely," the Contessa said with a reminiscent laugh.

"Pity we were photographed with two of the biggest arms dealers in Europe," said Desirée glumly. "This photograph would ruin me if it were ever published," she said, tearing it into little pieces. "Special envoys have to be above reproach, especially the heritage ones. Are you sure about the negatives?"

The Contessa nodded. "He says he put the five negatives in his safe the night before he was to bring them here. In the morning they were gone, along with other valuables which makes me hope that the thief didn't appreciate what their value was."

"Some hope that. As if a conman like Roberto

would keep innocent negatives in his safe. Who have you working for us?"

"Giulia, remember her, she works for Roberto. I have found her very satisfactory so far," replied the Contessa. She looked at Desirée. "Does this special envoy job mean that much to you?" she asked.

"You know it does. I love the life of a VIP, police escorts through cities, state receptions, fabulous cosmopolitan men. Of course I feel I'm doing so much for others too," was Desirée's emphatic reply.

"Then we must find those negatives!" The Contessa lit a cigarette. "How did Dublin go?" she asked.

"Oh very well, lunch with the President, reception – Dublin Castle, dinner – Leinster House and, of course, the Heritage Awards," replied Desirée smiling.

"Anyone recognise you?"

"I don't think so. One of the prize-winners was from a school we both know!"

"You're joking! Who was it?" asked the Contessa.

Desirée seemed amused. "Nuala O'Donnell from St Brigid's on the Boyne!"

The Contessa rose, looking for an ash-tray. "Oh her," she said crossly. "I might have guessed. She is always where she isn't meant to be."

2

Buon Giorno Roma

"How warm and sunny it is and it's only nine in the morning, too. I just know this Roman tour is going to be fun," enthused Josie as she walked out of the Basilica of St Mary Major with Eithne and Judith on the morning following their arrival in Rome.

"The weather is brilliant," agreed Judith. "Did you notice the blast of warm air that hit us when we got off the plane last night? I wish we had weather like this in Ireland, don't you, Eithne?"

"I do, of course. But I'm just mad we had to divide up, especially as we're stuck with those fifth years, not to mention the awful *Cleaner* woman."

Due to the incompetence of their tour operator, the forty-five girls from St Brigid's school, who had come on tour to Rome had to divide up into two parties on their arrival there. The bulk of them stayed in the original hotel, but some fifteen girls and two teachers had to go to a much smaller one tucked away in an old narrow street, on the Esquiline Hill not far from the Basilica of St Mary Major. To the relief of Nuala and Aileen, their own special friends were

10

included in these fifteen, plus Monica, Gwendoline and Deirdre. The rest were fifth years.

"I wouldn't mind so much if Sharon Kennedy and Lisa Shevlin weren't amongst them, they're bound to make trouble for us," continued Eithne gloomily.

"Cheer up," Josie said bracingly. "Miss Ryan is going to take us on our own, we're only going to join up with the others occasionally."

"It's a pity Gráinne and Ciara were kept with the main party," said Judith. "It won't be as nice for them as they'll be dumped in with the fourth years and Miss O'Brien."

"Did you hear that Gráinne is going to ring home this evening to find out what happened in *Together and Apart?*" laughed Josie. "She's a headcase."

"I hope we meet her then," said Judith, a keen fan of that popular soap. "I wouldn't mind hearing what happened myself."

They were now joined by Aileen and Nuala, who had come out of the Basilica behind them. "Just look at the birds," said Nuala, pointing to where dozens of pigeons strutted fearlessly around the piazza between the feet of the tourists there. "They walk around as if they own the place."

"Why not," said Aileen in a fair-minded way. "It's their city after all – we're the strangers, you know."

"Don't be an idiot, Aileen," laughed Judith. "I must take a few photographs of them, all the same."

Just then two people came across from a nearby shop and emptied a basket of bread on the ground near the pigeons. Within minutes the birds had swooped down and enthusiastically pounced on the food, rapidly gobbling it up. They all laughed at the sight of one pigeon flying lopsidedly off with a large loaf in his beak.

As the friends were watching with amusement the antics of the pigeons, in another part of Rome a small, slightly-built man was furtively examining the negatives which he had stolen some days earlier from his employer's safe. His large sad eyes, an invaluable asset to him all his life, gleamed and a small smile played around his lips, as he looked at the features of the people on the film. He was supposed to be engaged in folding smart fake suede jackets and placing them in glossy new plastic bags, which carried the famous name *Luichi* emblazoned in gold on them. Hearing someone coming, he had barely time to slip the films into a leather wallet, unusual in that it had two white birds embossed on it, before placing it in one of the pockets of the navy blue jacket he was folding. The door opened and a sharp-featured woman entered the room.

"Enrico," she said. "Roberto wants you at once." The man turned from arranging the long row of plastic bags.

"*Si*, Giulia," he replied humbly. "I'm coming, these are nearly ready now."

She held the door until he had left the room. Then closing it, she followed him to the office,

12

where an expensively-dressed dark-haired man was reading a newspaper. "*Buon giorno,* Enrico," he said, flicking over a coin to him. "Get me some cigarettes. I'll be in the car when you return."

"*Si,* boss," said Enrico, deftly catching the money and leaving the room.

Later on when Enrico had seen Roberto leave, he returned to the storeroom where to his dismayed surprise, the navy blue coat was missing. Looking sadder than ever, he sought out Giulia, making discreet enquiries as to its whereabouts.

"The navy blue jacket?" she repeated, looking thoughtfully at him. "If it was in the last row, Roberto took it with him. You know this is his day for working the *Via Cavour.*"

Back at the Basilica, Miss Ryan, the history teacher, was telling the third years the itinerary for the day. "First we're going to the church of *San Pietro* in Vincoli, where there is a very famous statue of Moses by Michelangelo, then we'll visit the Colosseum and in the evening the teachers have arranged for the whole group from St Brigid's to eat at a special restaurant together."

"Brilliant," said Josie. "We can compare notes on the places we've been to, not to mention hearing from Gráinne any news she may have about *Together and Apart.*"

"Miss Ryan," asked Monica. "This church we're going to, what does its name mean?"

"It means St Peter in chains," replied the teacher. "You may remember that St Peter was

13

imprisoned by King Herod in Jerusalem and then later on by the emperor in Rome. In each case, he was bound with chains, iron chains. The early Christians preserved these chains and they are now kept in a special shrine under the high altar in the church of that name. Is that all right, Monica?"

"Yes, thank you, Miss Ryan," said Monica.

"That reminds me, girls. I hope you brought your special notebooks to Rome as instructed. Each night I want you to write up your journal of the day's sightseeing. Don't forget the bascilica behind us. Remember, they started building it at the same time as St Patrick was travelling across Europe to bring the Good news to our ancestors."

"Oh no," complained Aileen. "That's much too much like school. Can't we just leave it to our prize-winning Nuala, she's good at that kind of thing."

"Certainly not, Aileen," laughed Miss Ryan. "I'll be looking forward to reading your account of this tour; maybe it will be the one we'll put in the school magazine, you never know."

Aileen made a face but said no more.

"It's the time for school tours, isn't it?" said Deirdre. "Look at the lines of children going into the bascilica. Judging by the coaches, I think they're German."

"Come on girls, we must go," said Miss Ryan hastily. "I don't want to get caught with them, that's why we left early."

"How can we cross the street?" asked Fidelma.

"There's millions of cars and they never seem to stop. I can't see any traffic lights either." She had been watching the hordes of heavy traffic go past in a seemingly unending stream while the others had been speaking to the teacher.

"I'll show you," said Miss Ryan, masterfully marshalling the girls and leading them over to the edge of the pavement. "Stand behind me and follow instantly when I raise my arm," she commanded. Waiting until she considered was a suitable moment, the teacher then held up her right arm, stepped boldly off the pavement and marched across the street. The timid girls obediently following her were relieved to see the whole row of vehicles stop short. As soon as the last pedestrian reached the other side, the traffic, as if released from bondage, swiftly swept past again with a great roar.

"I'll never mind Dublin traffic again, now that I've seen Roman," said Aileen. "It sounded just like a great wild beast as it passed behind us then."

"That was a brilliant display by Miss Ryan, wasn't it?" said Nuala. "I never thought she would have such great qualities in her."

"I didn't either," grinned Aileen. "I'll give a whole page in this painful journal we have to do, describing the incident. It will make her blush."

"You could head it 'She stopped the whole street with a wave of her hand'", said Nuala entering into the spirit of it. "Or maybe 'Irish teacher tames Roman traffic.'"

"Aren't the shops in this street, or should I call

it *via*, just full of interesting things to buy?" observed Josie, as they walked along enjoying the sun and discussing the all-important matter of presents for loved ones at home.

"It looks as if we won't have any trouble getting things for the Mumsies and Popsies after all," agreed Eithne. "Especially if you want leather, it's not too expensive here."

"Miss Grimes says the Vatican is the cheapest place for postcards," said Gwendoline.

As they were about to turn into the *Via Cavour*, Monica suddenly saw a handbag in one of the shop windows which she was convinced her mother would really love. Nothing would do for her but that she just had to go in and inquire the price. Gwendoline took out her phrase book, telling Monica as they went into the shop: "*Quanta costa* means how much does it cost?"

By dint of much pointing and other signs Monica eventually got the smiling assistant to produce the handbag for inspection. After a hasty confab with Gwendoline, who graciously approved, and a lot of fumbling in her money belt, Monica carefully counted out thirty-six thousand lira. Flushed with triumph she took her purchase and they left the shop together.

"There you are, thank goodness!" said Aileen appearing beside them on the crowded pavement, followed by an anxious-looking Nuala. "We have been looking for you all over. What were you doing?"

"I was helping Monica buy a beautiful leather

bag for her mum," replied Gwendoline. "Show it to them, Monica. A snip at eighteen pounds." Monica opened her parcel and proudly displayed her mother's present.

"It looks really super," approved Aileen. "But we'd better hurry before Miss Ryan misses us."

"You're lucky," explained Nuala. "Just as we noticed that you were gone, an old friend of Miss Ryan's turned up out of the blue. The pair of them are laughing and talking still, picking up the pieces, I suppose."

"Just as well the *Cleaner* isn't around," said Aileen. "She doesn't approve much of laughter, what would she think of laughing with a man?"

They caught up with the others just as Miss Ryan was introducing a tall man about her own age to them. "This is Felix Costello," she was saying. "We were at college together and these, Felix, are some of the third years I teach history to at St Brigid's."

"Hi, girls," said Felix, living up to his name by smiling in a happy way. "I hope she treats you well and doesn't behave like an old dragon too often."

"Don't be trying to undermine my authority," she reproved him laughingly. "You'd never guess he is supposed to be a sober lawyer, would you girls? Anyway, he's coming along with us until we reach the steps which will lead us up to the church of St Pietro."

They all set off then. Miss Ryan and her friend Felix in front with the girls at a discreet distance

17

behind them. Halfway down the *Via Cavour* a
large black car coming in the opposite direction
suddenly drew up, stopping at the pavement just
as the teacher and her friend were passing. There
was the sound of a car window winding down and
a plaintive voice called: "*Scusi*, could you help me,
please?"

3

The Coats, the Colosseum
and Constantine

They all stopped and stared at the black car, then
Miss Ryan, somewhat reluctantly followed by her
friend Felix, went over to see what she could do to
help. The occupant of the car, a dark-haired
expensively-dressed man, smiled genially at them
and produced a card which he waved vaguely
around.

"As you can see, " he said in a smooth foreign
accent, "I am the managing director of Armani in
Paris. I've just arrived from there today and I'm
lost. I wonder, could you help me."

It struck Vanessa Ryan that the accent didn't
sound remotely French.

"*Mamma mia*, what a terrible confusing city
Rome is," he said with a resigned laugh. "I'm
looking for the *Termini*."

"We are strangers here," said Felix, "but if you
drive to the top of the street and turn right past
the Basilica, you can't miss the *Termini*."

"Thank you, you are too kind, English perhaps?"

"No, not English," they stoutly denied. "We
are Irish, *Irlandaise*."

"Ah yes, of course. My wife is from Ireland. Now that you have been so kind, like all the Irish, I wish to give you a little present. In fact, I insist on it."

He leaned over to the back seat which they could see was crammed with glossy plastic bags, each one bearing the famous *Luichi* name on it. Pulling several of these bags on to the front seat, he produced a beautiful suede coat from one of them. Flipping the coat open he said urbanely. "These haven't been released to the shops as yet. As you can see they are beautifully finished and fully lined like all which bear the label *Luichi*. They will probably cost about £300 later on in the year, when they will be on sale in Dublin, but for you they are a present."

Vanessa stepped back saying: "No, no. I wouldn't dream of accepting such a gift."

"I insist," said the stranger, opening even more bags. "Ah yes, here is one that would suit the gentleman."

"It's very kind of you," said Vanessa, looking anxiously at Felix, "but I'm still not sure about taking it."

"If you feel that way," smiled the man in the car, producing at least a dozen credit cards from the top of the dashboard and spreading them out before them like a royal flush, "you could do another thing for me. As you can see I've plenty of these, but no loose lira, perhaps you could give me some." Adding "of course, if you have no money, it doesn't matter. Either way you must take your present. Please, I insist."

"Of course," said Vanessa, opening her money belt. "I'm sorry I haven't much, but you're welcome to it." And she pressed 25,000 lira into his hand.

The third years, who had been listening avidly to this exchange, now crowded around the car so that they could get a really good look at the famous *Luichi* coats. Eithne and Fidelma Murray in the front row were actually pressed against the car itself. Felix handed over his share, 20,000 lira, which he explained was the only spare cash he had on him, and the man rather grimly handed over two plastic bags, which the Murrays took and promptly passed back to Vanessa Ryan and her friend.

The stranger then said in a disappointed voice: "Only 20,000 lira, maybe the gentleman could find some more. My children were all born in Ireland," he paused and then asked, "What does the gentleman do for a living?"

"He is a lawyer," Fidelma informed him kindly and then as he was a foreigner, she felt he might not understand what this meant and added, "He prosecutes criminals, I think."

The effect on the managing director was magical. Instantly he started his car and within minutes he was speeding away up the *Via Cavour* and out of sight. A bewildered Vanessa Ryan and Felix Costello stood and looked at each other, then they both burst out laughing.

"There must be something wrong with these coats, no buttons or badly stitched," said Felix, taking his coat out of its pristine bag and trying it on. The coat, which was actually a stylish casual-type jacket, appeared to be perfect, every button in place with no sign of any faults whatsoever.

"That green suits you," said Vanessa Ryan. "I hope they're not stolen property."

"I doubt it, he probably thought we were wealthy tourists and would have plenty of money on us. On the other hand, I would say that the bags are fakes," was Felix's firm reply. "Anyway, it's a nice jacket and great value for £10."

Eithne lifted up the bag containing the other jacket. "This one is navy blue," she said. "I'll look after it for you, Miss Ryan. Fidelma and I have a huge case between us. I'll place this in the bottom of it. It'll be quite safe there."

"That would be great," said the teacher thankfully. "My case is quite small."

"We won't tell Miss Grimes about the coats or Mr Costello," said Monica loyally, if somewhat tactlessly.

"Talking about Miss Grimes, we must hurry up," replied Miss Ryan in repressive tones. "She wants us to meet them at the church and I don't want to keep her waiting."

With one accord they all started walking down the street again, discussing the whole coat affair excitedly.

When they reached the steps which would take them up to the church of *San Pietro* in Vincoli, Felix had to leave them. He gave Vanessa Ryan a card on which his Roman address and phone number were written, in case she wanted to get in touch with him. Then he said goodbye and went striding off down the street.

Nuala looked at the vegetation growing out of and sprawling over the cracked and broken steps they were climbing, as they followed Miss Ryan up through a tunnel which led to the top. "This place looks as ancient as it's supposed to be," she observed to Judith. "I wouldn't care to come here at night or even on my own during the day."

"My uncle Colum lent me his guide book," grinned Judith, "and it says that these stairs in their dark tunnel and the sinister door which opens out of it have all the atmosphere of ancient evil and intrigue."

"Wow, I wonder what went on here?" said Nuala impressed. "When you consider how old Rome is, I suppose loads of evil things have happened. I'm only glad these steps can't speak and tell us their story all the same."

Everyone was glad when they reached the top and could walk around in the lovely sunlight, where the church could be seen just to the left. Judging by the amount of coaches, cars and general noise around them, the girls soon realised that they were visiting a very popular tourist attraction. Miss Ryan gave them a comprehensive tour of the church paying special attention to St Peter's chains, then led them over to see the famous statue of Moses, undoubtedly the star draw. When she had left with the other girls, Nuala and Judith lingered for a last look at Michelangelo's masterpiece.

"It's some statue, isn't it," said Nuala.

"Simply brilliant," sighed Judith. "Imagine, Michelangelo was seventy years old when he finished it too. Just look at the way those veins stand out on the arms. He was a genius."

Eithne hurried over to them hissing in a low voice. "There's a big row going on out there. Apparently the fifth years were caught by the *Cleaner* chatting up guys at the Spanish Steps. Germans, I believe."

"You're joking," said Judith. "That crowd don't know a word of German."

"Probably they knew English," said Nuala. "How did you find out?"

Eithne laughed. "We all overheard Miss Grimes telling Miss Ryan. By the way, I was sent to get you two. I hope it means that we're going to have something to eat, I'm starving."

"You're always starving," retorted Judith. "Didn't you take your mother's advice and eat loads extra at breakfast?"

"I would have, only there wasn't loads to eat. Two rolls with some jam and coffee is not much of a breakfast," replied her cousin as they walked towards the church door.

"That's the continental breakfast, as the waiter kindly explained when someone asked for more," teased Nuala. "I'd say it was good for your figure, only you're so skinny already, you don't need to diet."

As they walked over to join Miss Ryan, the small rather bent figure of Miss Grimes passed them, followed by the fifth years, some of whom were looking extremely bad-tempered. Eithne swung the bag containing the suede jacket backwards and forwards.

"Did you see Lisa and Sharon, they looked murderous," she muttered to Judith who laughed and said: "Now we know which ones were talking to the boys."

"Where are we going to now, Miss Ryan?" asked Deirdre when everyone had gathered around the teacher.

Miss Ryan put away her map and smiled at them. "The Colosseum is next, Deirdre, then the arch of Constantine. They are all close together and quite near here, too."

"Then something to eat, I hope," said Fidelma firmly.

"Yes," agreed Eithne. "That continental breakfast almost makes me appreciate school food."

"I'd love an ice cream. Everyone says Italian ice cream is brilliant," said Josie.

"We'd better start moving then," said the teacher laughing, "before you all faint with hunger."

It didn't take long to reach the Colosseum, their only obstacle on the way being the usual heavy traffic which surged around it. Once safely across the street, they were free to wander around the enormous edifice. Despite their talk about hunger, the girls were most impressed by this ancient monument, listening with interest to Miss Ryan's brief history of it.

25

"Just imagine Nero having a colossal gold statue of himself one hundred and twenty feet high in his garden," said Aileen sometime later as they were walking towards the Arch of Constantine. "What an ego-tripper he was, and to think that is where the name Colosseum came from too!"

"Miss Ryan told it well, didn't she?" said Nuala. "I could just see the place packed with spectators cheering and roaring while the poor people were being torn to pieces by the lions."

"Just like the World Cup in a way," observed Josie flippantly. "Only of course it wasn't football exactly."

"I thought the bit about the sailors of the imperial fleet pulling across the big canvas sunshade, when the sun got too hot for comfort was very interesting," said Eithne. "I wonder did people go around selling food to the spectators?"

"I wouldn't be surprised," said Judith. "My guide book says that 50,000 people could fit into it, also that it had 80 exits, called *vomitoria*, so that everyone could leave quickly, if necessary."

"Yuk!" said Josie. "That guide book of yours is a bit much."

"*Vomitorium* only means exit, you dope," said Judith. "Think how neat it would sound if Sr Gobnait announced one morning; 'you may all leave now by the usual *vomitoria*'."

"That'll be the day," replied Josie, grinning in spite of herself.

They reached the Arch of Constantine where

Miss Ryan was impatiently waiting to tell them that it had been erected to commemorate the Emperor Constantine's victory over Maxentius in 312 AD. "Of course you all remember the famous story of Constantine having a vision, the night before the battle, of a huge cross in the sky and a voice saying: 'In this sign you shall conquer'," said Miss Ryan, looking hard at Gwendoline and Monica, who she felt weren't as interested as they might have been.

"I know that one, Miss Ryan, he was the first Christian emperor, wasn't he? He built lots of churches and was baptised only just before he died," said Gwendoline, startling everyone, but no one more so than the teacher, who hadn't expected such a response.

As they all walked away from the arch and down towards the Forum, Gwendoline said to Monica, "I bet you didn't think that I'd know about Constantine, did you? The fact is I had to learn about him one day in detention and it stuck in my mind. It was worth it to see the shock on Miss Ryan's face! And interesting to see his old arch too."

"What I notice about Rome is that everything is old and everyone is so famous," said Monica. "I'm really glad I came all the same."

"It's the sun, it preserves things, except your skin, of course," said Gwendoline earnestly. "It needs loads of moisturiser. I hope you have your sun block on."

"Absolutely," replied Monica. "Loads of it, just to be on the safe side."

It was Nuala who noticed the marble map on a wall near the Forum, showing the growth of the Roman empire from its beginnings. "Look," she cried, "there are four of these maps. Just see how the empire spread all over Europe."

They all stopped walking and looked with interest at the maps, pointing out the various countries to each other. "There's Ireland," said Judith. "That black one high up in front of England called Hibernia."

"Why is Ireland in black, when all the rest are white?" asked Deirdre.

"The white marble shows where the empire was established," explained the teacher. "As you know, Ireland was never conquered by Rome."

To her surprise a great cheer went up from the third years at this. "I'm afraid it was more of a case of Rome not bothering invading us, rather than us beating them back," she said, laughing at them.

"Makes no difference what the reason was," said Aileen.

"It's funny, isn't it," said Nuala. "How being away from home makes you feel so partisan."

"Yes," agreed Josie. "It brings out the patriot in us."

"I think it's time these patriots had something to eat," said the teacher.

"Cheers!" shouted Eithne and Fidelma together.

4

Trivia and Trevi

"What's that huge building we are passing now?" asked Judith, pointing to a resplendent white edifice with dozens of columns and crowned with sculptured black horses at each end.

"That's the Victor Emmanuel monument made of white marble. I believe it was nicknamed "the wedding cake" by allied troops in World War II," replied Miss Ryan.

"Well, it certainly sticks out," said Josie. "I suppose it's a kind of landmark, helps people not to get lost." Miss Ryan was very amused at Josie's practical use of this memorial dedicated to Italian independence.

The crowds moving slowly ahead of them came to a sudden stop. Aileen, Nuala and Judith, who were in front of the others, discovered that a long line of policemen was barring them from stepping off the pavement. There was a slight thinning of the crowd and the three girls found themselves pushed to the front row where they had a great view of the proceedings.

First of all a platoon of very colourfully dressed soldiers marched past, followed by a band playing a loud military air. They were followed by several soldiers stiffly carrying flags. There was a gap, then three black cars slowly passed, obviously carrying persons of some importance.

"Look, look," cried Nuala, pulling Aileen's arm in her excitement. "There in the second car, it's the special envoy we had at the prize-giving in Dublin, Madame something or other."

The two friends looked, just catching a glimpse of the tanned face of the passing envoy. "What a coincidence," said Judith. "Pity Josie didn't see her. She was so interested in hearing about her, if you remember."

Once the cavalcade had passed, the police just seemed to melt away. Then everyone was free to cross the street. Josie caught up with them as they reached the other side. "Did you see that woman?" she asked. "I've never seen anyone like her."

"What woman?" asked Nuala in a puzzled voice; surely Josie couldn't have recognised the special envoy.

"The policewoman, of course," replied Josie impatiently. "The one who was standing on a box in the street, directing traffic."

"A woman traffic cop, what's so unusual about that?" asked Aileen.

"Maybe you're used to traffic cops wearing very high heels, skirts up to their eyes and a face covered with make-up, but I'm not," retorted Josie in a sarcastic voice. "But could she direct traffic! She was brilliant even though she was quite old too."

"Wow, glamorous granny directing traffic, that's Rome for you," said Aileen, obviously impressed. "I'd like to see her."

"You can't," said Josie. "As I was staring at her, she hopped off the box, put on a crash-helmet, then got on a motor-bike and zoomed away, showing lots of leg."

Deirdre appeared out of the crowd.

"Come on, you lot. We've found a brilliant place to eat. It's just over there."

She turned and led the way. They surged joyfully behind her, needing no second invitation as their continental breakfast was only a faint memory by now. Miss Ryan and the rest of the party could be seen in a large café, queuing up before a long counter full of interesting-looking dishes of food.

"Aileen," said Nuala briskly. "You go along to the back of the café there and grab a table. I'll get yours, I know your tastes, we'll settle up later."

"Good idea," said Josie.

"You go with her, Judith. There's quite a crowd here already."

So it was arranged. Aileen and Judith commanded two tables, placing their bags on the chairs to warn anyone away. Nuala soon arrived with a loaded tray. "Chicken pieces, I think," she said rather breathlessly as she put it down. Removing several dishes from the tray, she placed them in front of Judith and Aileen. "Here you are, mushrooms, rice, beans and fried potatoes. Josie has the drinks and sweets. Help yourselves."

Judith removed her property from the chair next to her. "Sit here, Nuala," she said. She had already given the second table over to the grateful teacher, who had managed to get some extra chairs so that they all could fit together, even if it was a bit of a crush.

Josie appeared a minute later. "Here you are," she announced, "unfortunately, our favourite drink, *Jungle*, hasn't hit Rome yet. So I had to get something else, but it's really well chilled. Behold the *gelato* at last, that's ice cream, in case you don't know the lingo, Aileen."

"Thanks a million, Josie," said Aileen drily. "It'd better be good after all your talk about it," she warned.

Despite the fact that the food tasted quite different to what they were used to, they all enjoyed their meal. "That wasn't bad at all," said Josie, looking at their empty plates. "Different but tasty."

"Hunger is the best sauce," said Judith. "Now for the ice cream."

Maybe it was because they had looked forward so much to the ice cream, but they were disappointed when they came to eat it. "In fact," said Josie. "The ice cream is much nicer at home, I think."

"Cheaper too," agreed Nuala. "I wonder where we're going next."

"That reminds me," said Aileen. "It's time for a little crossword work, remember you promised to help."

"You didn't bring the ghastly things to Rome

with you, did you?" asked Nuala, aghast at the thought.

"Of course I did, and a very good idea it was of yours too. Don't worry, it's the last one, and I've only twenty-two clues left," replied Aileen, swiftly opening her bag and producing the dreaded crossword carefully contained in a plastic see-through cover. "Aristocratic title which originally meant companion, eight letters," read out Aileen looking hopefully at them.

"I haven't a clue," said Josie.

"What about 'A very large stretch of water'", said Aileen cheerfully, "five letters."

"Lake . . . pond . . . let me see . . . try ocean," said Judith.

"Brilliant, it fits and that gives me the second letter *a* for the next one."

"I must have been out of my mind when I suggested such a crazy idea to you, Aileen," groaned Nuala.

"'Food flavouring made from volatile oil of the climbing orchid, second letter *a*.'"

"You look like a dog begging for a biscuit, Aileen," said Josie. "What about peppermint?"

"Could it be almond, no, second letter is *a*. Vanilla, of course," suggested Nuala.

Aileen gleefully wrote *vanilla* in. "At this rate we'll be finished in no time," she said happily.

However, Miss Ryan rose from the table putting the others out of their agony.

"Please, Miss Ryan," said Gwendoline plaintively, when they were walking out of the restaurant. "Could we look at some shops now, as we visited two churches and several monuments already and it's still only our first day in Rome too."

Miss Ryan laughed. "I think we'll manage to fit in the shops today too," she said. "But first I want to take you to see the Trevi fountain. It's so famous and it has been cleaned up only lately too."

"Is that the *Three Coins in a Fountain* place?" asked Deirdre. "I saw the film on TV once."

"Yes," said the teacher, "but remember you must not throw coins in, it does terrible damage to the fountain."

"Fat chance," grinned Deirdre. "Everything is so expensive in this city, I've better uses for my coins."

It took nearly thirty minutes for them to reach the Trevi Fountain, as their progress was slowed down a lot by the crowds walking in the streets. They were all impressed at its size, gleaming pristine and white in its newly restored splendour, especially as it almost filled up the tiny piazza there. As usual in all these places, dozens of tourists were sitting around chatting, eating or taking photographs, enjoying their holiday in the sun.

"I have never seen such crystal clear water in my life," said Nuala, looking at it as it sparkled, foamed and gushed its way over the rocks and into the huge basin below, the bottom of which could be seen clearly by everyone.

"Roman water is famous," said Miss Ryan. "It's

been coming into the city through acqueducts since the days of the empire, in fact they were considered one of the wonders of the ancient world."

"The Romans must have been great engineers," said Judith.

"They were. According to the guide book, at the fall of Rome, when the barbarians sacked it, they destroyed the acqueducts and all through the middle ages Romans suffered from a lack of water," said Miss Ryan. "Then the popes had some of the acqueducts restored and, to celebrate this happy event, the fountains were built."

"Does your guide book explain what these figures represent, Miss Ryan?" asked Deirdre, pointing at the sculptured figures in the niches on either side of the central arch.

"Yes, it does. The male figure in the shell is Oceanus riding through the arch, pulled by tritons and two seahorses, one tamed and one untamed to symbolise calm and rough waters. The four females figures represent the four seasons of the year."

"Well it certainly won't be your fault, Miss Ryan, if we come back knowing nothing," said Monica, to the great amusement of the other girls.

"Thank you, Monica," laughed the teacher. "I'm glad you appreciate my efforts."

They sat down to enjoy the sun but not for long. The Murrays, discovering a nearby shop selling attractive leather goods with prices clearly displayed on each item in the window, hurried over to ask permission from the teacher to do some shopping there. The visit to the shop gave great satisfaction as everything in it was attractive and quite moderately priced.

"The worry of getting presents to take home quite spoils holidays," complained Judith as she surveyed two wallets, one black and one brown, trying to decide which was the more attractive.

"They are both nice," advised Eithne, having been consulted. "But I think the brown one has the edge."

"You're probably right," agreed Judith. "I'll take it and I think that blue purse as well."

"We got a couple of those bracelets, you know the plaited leather ones and some very special hair ornaments," said Eithne in a pleased voice.

Josie joined them. "Miss Ryan wants to know are you ready to leave. Did you see the brooch Nuala got for her mum, it's a sweet little gold kingfisher, with blue and green flashing wings. I got a brilliant belt for my sister, she'll love it, I know."

"I'm coming," said Judith. "I was just waiting for my change."

Miss Ryan was waiting outside the shop, looking a bit flustered. "I wasn't as unselfish as the rest of you," she confessed. "The leather was so cheap, I bought a lovely suede bag to match that jacket I acquired this morning."

"It's so hot," said Gwendoline. "In fact, I think it's even hotter than when we went into that shop."

"I agree with you, Gwendoline," said the teacher. "We'll walk along until we see one of those cafés where you can sit outside underneath umbrellas and we'll have a rest and a nice cool drink.

They hadn't to walk very far along the street before Josie called their attention to what they were looking for. Unfortunately, a lot of other people seemed to have had the same idea and all the outside tables had been taken already. However they went into the café as everyone felt very thirsty, taking over a long banquette at the wall facing the window. They had hardly sat down when a sudden vivid jag of lightning lit up the café, quickly followed by a heavy roll of thunder. They all stared as a veritable sheet of heavy rain poured down, obscuring their view.

"I hope those umbrellas are waterproof," said Josie. "Weren't we lucky that there was no room for us outside!"

"They aren't waterproof," said Fidelma. "Look at the people crowding in the doorways."

The thunder, lightning and heavy rain lasted about fifteen minutes, then it was all over. The sun shone down as if nothing had happened. The third years, who were finished their refreshments by now, got up and left. Once out in the street, they were amazed to see that except for a slight steam issuing from the ground, which soon dispersed, there was no sign that it had ever rained, except that the air was slightly fresher.

"Miss Ryan," said Aileen, sidling up to her, as

37

they all walked along. "Do you know which aristocratic title originally meant 'companion'?"

"No Aileen, I can't say I do. Why do you ask, is it important?" replied the puzzled teacher.

"Oh no, not at all," replied Aileen vaguely. "It's just something I often wonder about."

5

Restaurants and Rendezvous

Nuala and Judith walked slowly along the narrow street leading from the hotel, enjoying the warm evening air. They were alone as the rest of their group were still taking it easy after the strenuous day they had spent sightseeing and shopping, not to mention walking all the way back to their hotel, which was near the top of the Esquiline hill.

"This whole place just looks like the description in our history book of a medieval street," Nuala was saying enthusiastically. "Narrow and cobbled, tall houses with shuttered windows with people living above the shops. Look at the shops too, shoemakers, artists, bakers, jewellers."

"That one is selling fresh pasta and nothing else," Judith pointed out.

"The one beside it sells wine. I could imagine Romeo meeting Juliet in such a street as this," said Nuala soulfully.

"I'd agree with you," replied Judith, laughing, "if it wasn't for the long line of cars parked all along one side of the street. It quite spoils the image, doesn't it? Very modern cars too."

"Those cars have lots of dents in them," said Nuala, coming down from the heights.

"I can't say I'm surprised, when you see the way the traffic speeds down this narrow street all day and most of the night," said Judith. "Did you notice it last night?"

"I certainly did. I suppose it sounds so bad because the street is so narrow that the sound rises up to us on the top floor."

At that the two girls had to jump off the street and into a shop entrance to avoid the two or maybe three cars they could see racing in their direction.

"There's Josie," said Nuala, spotting their friend coming out of the hotel and looking down the street in their direction. "I wonder what she's up to."

She waved and Josie hurried down to meet them. "Hi Nuala, hi Judith," she said. "Miss Ryan wants us to assemble inside the door of the hotel. The coach with the rest of St Brigid's is expected any minute."

"Great," replied Judith. "Miss Ryan says that this restaurant we are going to is something special."

"It will be nice to meet Gráinne and Ciara," said Nuala. "It's a pity we had to split up."

"Yes," agreed Judith. "I hope Gráinne has some news about *Together and Apart*."

"We turned on the TV here and you wouldn't believe what was on," said Josie. "*Robin Hood!* The ancient film with someone called Errol Flynn as

40

Robin. It was deadly, especially as it was all in Italian. Robin said *'Magnifico'* a few times which was all I could understand anyway."

Aileen met them at the door of the hotel. "You missed the briefing session," she told them. "The whole crowd of us will be sitting at one long table in this place we are going to. Remember, no shouting or rude remarks about the food. And whatever happens, speaking to members of the opposite sex is *absolutely forbidden!*"

"I hope we don't meet anyone we know, it could be very awkward. St Paul's school, Navan, are supposed to be doing their tour this week too," said Josie, chuckling.

"You could always talk to the girls and explain the ban to them. It's a mixed school, isn't it?" said Aileen.

"I'm more worried about the waiters: when they ask what we want to eat, we'll all have to pretend to be deaf and dumb," said Judith.

It wasn't long before the coach with the main party arrived. As they all piled in, followed by the two teachers, they were greeted affectionately as if they had been separated from them for two months instead of a mere twenty-four hours. Speeding through the city streets, they were soon deposited at a restaurant whose name, *La Grotta Azzurra*, was flashing on and off in neon lights. Obviously a popular spot if the rows of empty coaches lining the street in front of it were anything to go by.

An unpretentious entrance led into a narrow

room, whose walls had been painted to resemble the sea, with a variety of birds flying over white-capped waves. At the far end of this room, an upturned fishing boat could be seen draped in nets which also hung from black rocks flanking the cave-like opening. When the excited girls passed through this they found themselves in an enormous dining-room decorated to look like a cavern under the sea. Huge-eyed monsters of the deep goggled at them from walls lavishly decorated with seaweed. Dozens of candlelit tables, covered in starched white cloth, gleamed ghostly under the blue lights playing over everything. At the rear of the room, an energetic band belting out music popular several decades previously competed with the din caused by dozens of people eating, talking and laughing cheerfully.

The head waiter hurried forward, all smiles. "*Buona sera signore, mesdames,* leddies." In no time the slightly bemused St Brigid's party were sitting at a long table along one side of the large dining-room, while several waiters complete with menus came forward to receive their orders.

Although the service was excellent, and the food pleasant, it wasn't until they were eating their main course that anyone felt like talking, as the accumulative noise of a great many people in the room, combined with the loud music from the band, was quite deafening. After a frustrating attempt to discover from Gráinne, sitting opposite her, how she had spent her first day in Rome,

Aileen gave up the struggle. Furtively slipping her crossword puzzle in its plastic cover on to the table, she whispered in Nuala's ear: "Large wolf-like breed of dog also called German Shepherd. Eight letters."

Nuala took a forkful of chicken and rice and ate it thoughtfully. "Alsatian," she replied.

Aileen gave a pleased yip and quickly filled in the word. Then she said in a low voice: "Capital of Sicily, seven letters ending in O".

Nuala shook her head. "Aileen," she said. "How did you do the other crosswords if you have to ask me all this one? I don't know, honestly I don't."

"It's Rome, I just can't think here. I'll put it away, I know it's not really fair," Aileen replied, putting it away in her bag, looking a bit like a dog who has been refused a biscuit by his master. Nuala, feeling a monster, relented.

"If I remember it, I'll tell you, but try and forget the challenge for tonight, please."

Just then the band stopped playing, creating a welcome lull in the noise for a moment or two. Judith, quickly seizing her chance, asked Gráinne if she had heard any news about *Together and Apart*.

"I have," replied Gráinne triumphantly. "I had to ring my mother, so I found out Phoebe is still trying to decide whether to run away or not. Andrew saw Josh outside the diner burning something of Candy's, maybe her history project, also it's raining at home."

43

"Brilliant," said Judith. "But not about the rain of course. When will you hear next?"

"I'm not sure," replied Gráinne. "But I may ring again in a few days' time. It's not too expensive if you use a public phone box, the hotel charges a bomb though."

"Where did your crowd go to today?" asked Eithne.

"We went with Miss O'Brien to the Basilica of St John Lateran, after that San Clemente. It's a very ancient church run by Irish Dominicans. We all went down underneath the church to see the original Basilica of San Clemente. He was an early pope, fourth I think. Anyway, underneath that they found a second century shrine to some pagan god or other. It was spooky."

The band started up again, drowning further conversation. However, this time a pleasant tenor voice could be heard singing: "Be my love and I'll never more forget you" or words to that effect. The song floated across the room, followed by another song which appeared to be about saying goodbye to Rome. This second one was very popular with one large group of tourists, who kept asking for it. Miss Grimes at the top of the table looked pleased and explained to the girls and teachers near her, that these were the pop songs of her youth, which didn't surprise anyone.

The singer came nearer and nearer to their table, then he stopped. Josie swivelled around in her seat to get a better view and saw him talking to Miss Grimes. "Wow, she must be asking him to

44

sing something for her," Josie whispered. "He has such sad eyes too, you could only feel sorry for him, especially when you see the little box he carries, for tips, I suppose."

The next minute he was singing again, only this time it was something about seeing a stranger across a crowded room, which had an unsettling effect on most of the girls, especially Josie and those around her.

"Once you have found her, never let her go," he sang plaintively at the St Brigid's table, as he walked along one side of it.

"I like that!" growled Aileen. "After all her talk about never speaking to the opposite sex!"

"Once you have found him, never let him go," pleaded the sad-eyed singer, passing down the other side.

"Excellent advice," hissed Josie. "Pity she can't take it herself."

"Easier said than done," whispered Eithne back, making a horrible face at Josie as she did so.

Gráinne, catching sight of this face, had a terrible desire to laugh, then looking at the singer tried to stop, which caused the laugh to turn into an unexpected loud snort, startling everyone around her. At that the whole table was convulsed with laughter, which they tried vainly to suppress.

As soon as the song was finished an embarrassed Gráinne struggling to regain her composure quickly asked Nuala a question about the places they had visited that day. Nuala, still chuckling, started to tell her about their visit to the Church of St Peter in Chains, not forgetting the extraordinary event which happened to them on the *Via Cavour* on their way to the ancient steps.

"Why would a stranger make a present of suede coats to Miss Ryan and her friend?" Gráinne asked in amazement. "There must be something wrong with them."

"We thought that too," said Nuala. "But we couldn't find anything wrong with them. They are in impressive glossy *Luichi* bags too and Miss Ryan's is a beautiful navy blue."

Nobody noticed that the sad eyed singer was standing close behind their table, listening avidly to Nuala's story of the coats.

"I wish I was with you lot," said Gráinne. "You have such fun. We have to trail around with the fourth years and it's not the same."

"I wish you were too," said Josie. "But remember we have the *Cleaner* with us, though to be honest, she hasn't bothered us much yet."

"Give her time," laughed Eithne. "We've been in Rome only one day, you know."

"We did so much today," said Judith. "I wonder what plans Miss Ryan has for tomorrow."

"The Spanish Steps is one of them, I know," said Aileen. "But I don't know any more than that."

"There's a McDonald's near the Spanish Steps," said Fidelma. "Civilisation at last. That's one place I'll be sightseeing tomorrow."

"You are a barbarian, Fidelma," said Judith in

mock reproof. "You only think of your stomach. Rome is simply full of art and ancient beauty and all you look forward to is Big Macs and chips. I'm ashamed of you."

Fidelma wasn't the slightest bit impressed, she only laughed at her art-loving cousin.

Soon it was time for them to leave. As they passed back through the cave entrance the strains of '*Arrivederci Roma*, Goodbye Rome' floated across to them.

"He's still singing that one," commented Judith to Josie, who said: "He sounds a lot happier, maybe the tips are good tonight."

"That song," said Aileen. "He must be sick of it, he sang it at least fifty times tonight."

"I'm sure he doesn't mind," said Josie. "As long as the tourists cross his palms with lots of lovely *lira*."

"Palms, palms, what does that remind me of?" said Nuala. "I know, Palermo, I think it's the capital of Sicily."

"Brilliant," cried Aileen. "That means we've only about eighteen left to do."

"Who are *we*?" asked Nuala. "You're the one who rashly took on the competition."

"I know, Nuala, but you all promised to help and you're so brilliant too," said Aileen, smiling in what she hoped was a winning way.

"I hope you will be as eager to share the winnings," said Nuala, grinning in spite of herself.

"Remember it was me who got Mars, four letters, god of war," Josie reminded her. "If you win that weekend in Galway, I expect at least six hours in the hotel as my share."

"Six hours, you must be joking," retorted Aileen. "Mars, god of war, four letters would be considered a six-minute share at the very most."

"Well, if that's your attitude, Aileen," said Josie haughtily as they got into the coach, "I shall not proffer my valuable assistance for those last eighteen clues. You will be sorry, I promise."

6

Surprises on the Steps

"That was a good place we went to last night, Vanessa, wasn't it? I must say I enjoyed it," said Miss Grimes. She was sitting in front of the mirror in her room, putting the finishing touches to her appearance. It was nearly eight in the morning following the visit to *La Grotto Azzurra*.

Vanessa Ryan frowned slightly, choosing her words carefully, having no wish to offend her colleague. "I found it a bit too touristy," she said at last. "The food was all right, but not special. I think I'll take my group to somewhere more traditional tonight."

"Good idea," replied the older teacher. "I've arranged with Kitty O'Brien to go to a place she knows near the main hotel. You don't mind, do you?"

"No, Dottie, not at all. I am taking my lot down to the Spanish Steps today, and I don't expect to be back before 6 p.m. I'll see you then," said Vanessa, preparing to leave the room.

Dottie swung around in her seat. "Vanessa," she said earnestly. "Be vigilant at the Spanish Steps. As you know, we'd barely arrived there yesterday, when I found Lisa Shevlin and Sharon Kennedy being chatted up, I think the expression is, by two boys, German I believe. You never know where that could have led to."

Vanessa laughed at the expression on the other woman's face. "I'll be careful, you needn't worry," she said, wondering what Dottie would make of her adventure of the previous day with Felix Costello on the *Via Cavour*.

"You think I'm making a fuss about nothing, don't you," cried Dottie. "I must tell you about my friend, who teaches in a Dublin school. They took a group to Paris from her school one year. The day they arrived, before they had even got out of the coach, they stopped for a few minutes in the *Place de la Concorde*. Their coach drew up beside another one with Italian schoolboys in it. Mark this, nobody got out of either coach. Late that night a group of these boys turned up at the hotel claiming that the girls had given them the name of their hotel and had invited them to come and see them there. They were very persistent too, I believe."

"You're not serious. What did your friend do?" asked Vanessa.

"She didn't have to do anything. The concierge sent for the police and they got rid of them fast."

"How dreadful. I'll be on my guard," promised Vanessa, as she left the room, not that she was really worried, as she didn't believe any of her group would invite strange boys back to their hotel or get involved in anything they shouldn't.

50

In consequence she was quite shocked on entering the hotel restaurant, a room depressingly decorated in brown and orange stripes, to find the two Murrays, Gwendoline and Monica, threatening the waiter with some awful punishment if he didn't bring them a double helping of bread rolls, pronto.

"Girls," she called sternly, grateful that there were no other guests present. "Whatever are you doing? Please behave yourselves."

The waiter, who bore a strong resemblance to the emperor Nero, came over to her with a friendly *'Buon giorno'*.

"*Buon giorno*, some orange juice and black coffee, please."

"*Si signoria*." He went off, returning shortly not only with her order but with a large basket of rolls and croissants, which he placed in front of the girls, saying, "Continental breakfast, *si*."

"*Grazie, grazie,*" they said, feeling very pleased with themselves.

"You see," said Eithne, "it worked."

The room began to fill up with other guests and the rest of St Brigid's, so the teacher reserved her remarks for another time, especially as she was now joined at the table by Miss Grimes.

"It was only fun," explained Eithne, when they were being interviewed by Miss Ryan later in their room. "He knew that we didn't mean any harm."

"Please don't do it again. Remember we represent Ireland and we don't want to give people a bad impression of our country."

51

"I don't think the Romans have even heard of Ireland," said Gwendoline. "They all think we ar *Inglese* or *Americano*, anyway."

"I don't know about that, Gwendoline," replied Miss Ryan sternly. "But you can be sure if you do anything wrong, everyone will know that you're Irish. I'll be ready in ten minutes, then we'll set off for the Spanish Steps.

"What did you say to him?" asked Judith, after the teacher had left and they were all going down in the lift.

"Nothing much really. I only said that we would have him trussed up and thrown into the Tiber, if he didn't give us enough to eat."

"Wow, you must have been hungry," said Judith.

"I don't think he understood a word I was saying, it was just bad luck V Ryan coming in and hearing," replied Eithne, not looking noticeably worried.

"He got the message all the same, I believe," said Fidelma. "I hope he remembers it again tomorrow morning."

The teacher was as good as her word and within fifteen minutes they were passing the Basilica of St Mary Major, and walking along one of the streets leading away from it. *"Via Depretis,"* Nuala read from a plaque on the wall above a shop, at the street corner. "Does this street go all the way to the steps, Miss Ryan?"

"In a way it does, but it changes its name as it goes along. First it becomes *Via Della Quattro*

Fontanes on account of the fountains that are on each corner, where it is crossed by another street. Later on it becomes *Via Sistina* after Pope Sixtus V, who built it."

Their progress was slow, due as much to the incredibly bad condition of the cracked and broken pavements, as to the crowds of people passing along them. However, it was still good fun, walking downhill in the sun with lots of interesting things to see in the shops along the way. Needless to remark, as usual, the traffic roared past as it it were doing the last lap of the Monte Carlo motor race.

They barely glanced at the four fountains, which Miss Ryan told them were dedicated to the rivers Tiber and Arno and the goddesses Diana and Juno, as they were so keen to get to the famous Spanish Steps. Arriving at the *Via Sistina* they found that they were going uphill again, eventually finding themselves at the base of a long flight of wide stone steps. Everyone else seemed to be going up these steps, so immediately Miss Ryan and the girls followed them up.

There was a wide stone parapet at the top of the staircase and the now rather breathless group thankfully joined the other people leaning on it. A most wonderful panorama of Rome was their reward. Murmers of appreciation came from all of them. "Wow," said Aileen. "That's some view of Rome, I only wish I knew which was what."

She was interrupted by Josie, who pointed to the view beneath the parapet. "Look down there," she cried. "There's a simply huge flight of steps going down from here on both sides with palm trees and flowers and loads of people walking up them."

They all looked to where she was pointing. "They must be the Spanish Steps," said Judith. "What a brilliant way to see them."

"Yes," agreed Josie. "All the pictures show the steps from the street side up. I must have a photo of it."

"I must say I'm glad we're going down not up," said Monica to Gwendoline, who agreed fervently. "There are millions of steps and we'll have that long walk back to the hotel. I really think Miss Ryan overdoes the walking, don't you? The others go everywhere by coach."

To the girls' surprise Miss Ryan didn't seem interested in the famous steps. something else was obviously worrying her. "The church of the *Trinita dei Monti* should be around here," they heard her say. "But I can't see it anywhere."

Nuala looked around to where an enormous church loomed just behind them. "Could it be that one there with the twin towers?" she asked the teacher.

Miss Ryan turned swiftly around and gave a rueful laugh. "I feel such an idiot," she confessed. "Here was I looking all over Rome for it and all the time it was just behind us."

"What's so special about this church?" asked Eithne, wondering if it was too early to mention McDonald's to the teacher.

"It's not really the church I want, it's the

convent attached to it," replied the teacher. "There's a miraculous painting of Our Lady there which I would very much like to see. I've seen copies of it of course, but it's never the same as the original."

This sounded intriguing and they all agreed that they would like to see this painting too. So they went back to the church, eventually finding the convent door. Once inside they met a nun whose English was about as good as their Italian, but once Miss Ryan mentioned the miraculous picture she understood and swiftly showed the way to it saying, "Capella Mater Admirabilis."

As they walked up the stairs to the corridor where the painting was to be found, Miss Ryan explained that it had been painted for the benefit of the junior children of the then school. In consequence it was painted on the wall of an ordinary school corridor and quite low down too. This sounded unusual but, when they turned into the corridor, it hadn't prepared them for the sweet-faced girl painted in glowing colours on the wall in front of them.

"Wow," said Josie in a low voice. "She's so young and look at her hair – curls. I've never seen Our Blessed Lady with curls before."

Miss Ryan laughed. "It caused comment at the time too, also the colour of her dress."

"It's a lovely pink," said Nuala. "What was wrong with that?"

"Well, some people thought that it was a bit frivolous for the Madonna; blue was the normal colour or white, I think. The painter used the junior school uniform as a model."

"Look at the date, 1844. I can't believe it," said Judith. "The colours are so fresh, it looks as if it was only painted yesterday."

"It's a fresco," said Miss Ryan. "That means it's painted on fresh plaster, so that when it dries it becomes part of the wall."

"It's beautiful," said Aileen. "I'm glad you brought us here to see it," a sentiment with which all the other girls agreed.

"I'm so glad, it's even better than I had anticipated," said Miss Ryan.

They knelt down on the benches in the little chapel and prayed silently for a minute before trooping out again, saying *grazie* and goodbye to the little nun at the door.

They enjoyed the walk down the famous steps, admiring the flowers and the holiday atmosphere which rose up from the people enjoying the sun in the *Piazza di Spagne*. Miss Ryan had just pointed out the fountain of the barge to them in the piazza and was about to tell them its history when Josie gave a screech.

"Look, there are stalls down there selling things. We must go and look at them," she cried.

"T-shirts," cried Nuala. "That's what they sell. My brother went inter-railing last summer. He told me the ones here were the cheapest in Europe."

Before the teacher could say a word, the whole lot of them ran down the last few remaining steps to investigate the goods and were soon lost in the crowd milling around the stalls. The clamour and din there was terrific with at least a dozen Italian voices loudly inviting everyone to come and buy their wares. One of the vendors, a girl, thrust a large white T-shirt with *Roma* inscribed above a picture of the Colosseum at Josie and Judith. "Very large," she cried harshly. Holding up two fingers she added, "Two for 15,000 liras only. Very good value."

"£2.50 a pair, not bad at all and look at the size of them. I'll get a few," said Josie to Judith, who agreed heartily with her. The rest of the girls felt the same and within ten minutes the jubilant group were standing in the centre of the piazza inviting trouble from the passing traffic, especially as they were in the path of a busy taxi rank, discussing their spoils.

"I got two Colosseum and two Trevi Fountain," said Eithne. "What did you buy, Judith?"

"Two each of the Spanish Steps, Sistine Chapel and the Colosseum," replied her cousin in a pleased voice. "The Sistine Chapel one has the part where the hands of God and Man are just meeting. I think it's the best."

"We'd better move away from here," said Miss Ryan. "I think a taxi is trying to pass. We'll go for something to eat. I suppose you are all hungry as usual."

"Great," said Fidelma. "And I know the very place, Miss Ryan. It's called *McDonald's* and it's just over there, see the famous sign."

7

Migraine and Men

As it was still quite early they didn't have to queue for long in McDonald's. Soon they were all sitting together in a quiet corner eating their lunch. "Real food at last," said Eithne thankfully, as she lifted a forkful of golden chips to her mouth.

Miss Ryan shook her head sadly. "How could you, Eithne?" she reproved. "I see I'll have to take you to a *trattoria* for some real Italian cooking, considered by many as the best in the world."

Eithne, looking sceptical, just went on eating her chips. "Miss Ryan," asked Aileen. "Do you know the name of a legendary Greek king and hero of a work by Homer?"

The teacher was taken aback. "Are you sure you're feeling all right, Aileen?" she asked, making everyone laugh. "Homer mentions several Greek kings, Menelaus, Agememnon. I know, it's Odysseus, of course."

"Thank you, Miss Ryan," said Aileen gratefully. "I'm sure you're right. The only thing is, how do you spell that name?"

Miss Ryan, looking surprised, spelled "Odysseus". When Aileen had scribbled it down, the teacher said, "Why are you so interested in Homer all of a sudden?"

Aileen looked nonplussed for a second, then she said mysteriously, "I'm afraid you'll have to wait until you're reading my Roman journal, then all will be revealed to you."

Miss Ryan laughed. "I'll be looking forward to reading that," she promised. "I'm glad you're writing it up. I hope the rest of you are too."

Above the chorus of yeses, Monica's voice could be heard, "I hope you're not too fussy about spelling," she said. "Some of these places we go to have such weird names."

"What have you planned for us next?" asked Nuala, when Miss Ryan had reassured Monica about the spellings.

"I'll show you," replied the teacher, taking out her map of Rome and spreading it on the table in front of them. "This is where are now," she said, pointing to the place marked *Piazza di Spagna*. Her finger moved slowly to the right and along the map to *Piazza del Popolo*. "This is where we will be going next as you can see, it's not very far away."

They all craned to see the map. "It's a very big *piazza*," said Aileen. "What does *piazza* mean?"

"It means square. It is big with fountains and a huge obelisk in the centre, which Augustus brought from Heliopolis where it was built in the 13th century BC."

"Wow," said Nuala. "Nearly three thousand three hundred years ago. I must see that."

"Is that why we are going there," asked Judith, "to look at the obelisk?"

"Not really, there is something there you'd really appreciate Judith. The church, *Santa Maria del Popolo*, is a veritable treasure-house of artistic achievements. Raphael, Caravaggio and Pinturicchio are just a few of the famous artists who helped to decorate this church."

"Great," said Judith, who liked the art works best of all on the tour.

Miss Ryan smiled. "And for those of you who are more interested in the human side: the church was originally built over Nero's tomb in an effort to exorcise his ghost which was reputed to haunt the area, which must have been most unpleasant for the locals."

They got up to go. As Miss Ryan was putting away her map, she noticed Gwendoline near her. "Gwendoline," she said. "I forgot to tell you, we'll be passing *Via Condotti* and *Via Babuini*, where the most fashionable boutiques in Rome are to be found."

"Oh Miss Ryan, how brilliant," said Gwendoline, rushing over to tell Monica the good news.

As they left the restaurant, refreshed for the moment, Aileen said to Nuala; "That's only eighteen left. I've got one myself this time. The capital of the state of Arizona must be Phoenix, which makes it only seventeen."

"Brilliant Aileen. I bet you'll get it done in no time," replied a relieved Nuala.

While Miss Ryan and the third years were passing through a lively fruit market some time later, on their way to the *Piazza del Popolo*, in another part of the city Miss Grimes felt her head beginning to ache. Earlier that day she and the fifth years had joined up with the main party on a visit to the Catacombs. It was when she was getting into the coach again, after several hours sightseeing, that her eyes became affected.

"I'm afraid I'm in for a bad bout of migraine," she told Miss O'Brien, one of the other teachers present.

"Poor Dottie, you'll just have to go back to your hotel and lie down. Don't worry, I'll look after the fifth years for you," said Miss O'Brien in quick sympathy.

When the coach arrived back at the hotel, Miss O'Brien asked, "Will you be all right on your own?"

"I will, of course, A couple of hours in a darkened room usually does the trick," replied Miss Grimes as she alighted from the coach.

"We'll be back to pick you up for the evening meal. Take care," said Miss O'Brien with a final wave as the coach drove away.

A few hours later the English teacher awoke from a refreshing sleep, feeling so much better that she decided to get up and go up to the roof garden of the hotel.

Collecting sunglasses and a book, she left the room, almost bumping into a man who was standing just outside her door.

"Scusi, signora," he said politely. "Are you Miss Ryan?"

"No, no." she answered. "I am Miss Grimes, Miss Ryan is not back yet. Can I help you?"

The man hesitated then he replied, "I have been sent to collect her suede jacket, it has something wrong with it."

Miss Grimes frowned, as far as she knew Vanessa didn't have a suede jacket with her. It was the wrong time of year for suede anyway. "I don't know anything about it," she said. "You'd better come back later on this evening, when she is here herself."

He looked sadly at her, this reminded her instantly of the singer in *La Grotta Azzuria*. "Surely I've seen you before," she said sharply. "Aren't you the singer in that restaurant we were at last night? You are very like him."

"No, no, you mix me up with someone else," he protested. "I come back tonight when the other teacher is here."

"You do that," she replied, very carefully locking the bedroom door.

"Si, signora," he said quietly and went away. She went off to the roof garden where she soon established herself comfortably in a reclining chair under a large umbrella.

Enrico, for of course it was he, left the hotel and walked rapidly down the narrow street, never noticing Giulia staring at him from the shoemakers. As soon as he had passed the shop, she grabbed her purchases and set off after him.

Several hours later Miss Ryan and the third

years arrived back in the hotel again, just as Miss Grimes and her gang were leaving in the St Brigid's's coach. At the last minute Gráinne and Ciara received permission to stay for the evening with the other third years in the small hotel. They were warmly welcomed by Aileen and Josie who came down to escort them up to meet the others. "We're going to our room," Aileen informed them. "Everyone is in there for a bit of nosh."

Gráinne and Ciara were delighted to hear this. "Where did you go today?" Gráinne asked as they were going up in the lift.

"Anything exciting happen?" asked Ciara, remembering the incident of the suede coats on the previous day.

"Well, first of all we walked down to the Spanish Steps," said Aileen. "Followed by the best chips in town at good old McD's. Then we went to see this church absolutely stuffed with art. Judith went wild and had to be restrained there."

"I liked the frescoes myself," said Josie. "There was a super one of the Nativity. I suppose you know what a fresco is, girls? That's the advantage of Miss Ryan, she explains everything."

"She's good fun too," said Ciara. "You're lucky. Miss O'Brien is all right, but it's not the same."

"I love Rome," said Gráinne. "There's so much to see. We went to the Catacombs today. They were brilliant."

"How's the crossword coming on, Aileen?" asked Ciara. "Will you get it finished in time, do you think?"

"Nicely, thanks. I've only seventeen puzzles left to do, but they are real brutes. Would either of you like to try and solve them for me?" asked Aileen hopefully.

"No, thanks. I'm hopeless at crosswords," said Gráinne, as they got out of the lift, letting Aileen lead the way.

When Aileen opened her door, they were met by a burst of chatter and laughter. The room seemed to be packed with girls, sitting on chairs, beds and even the floor. "Come in, come in," called Nuala hospitably. "Move up there, Judith and make room for our guests."

"Yes ma'am!" said Judith cheerfully. "She's so bossy, because Miss Ryan put her in charge of us this evening."

"What's wrong with Miss Ryan?" asked Gráinne, as she squeezed in between Judith and Gwendoline.

"Nothing, she's just relaxing in her room for an hour or so."

Then Eithne passed around a basket of simply enormous plums, advising everyone to protect themselves with the tissues provided. "Where did you get these monsters?" asked Ciara. "They are juicy."

"When we left the Spanish Steps we walked through a street where there was a market selling almost everything," replied Judith. "So we bought some of the fruit. The plums are big, all right."

"Yes," said Fidelma, "and very sweet too," as she mopped her hand and face.

"Do you walk everywhere?" asked Gráinne. "We are taken by coach all the time."

"Miss Ryan thinks it's the only way to get to know Rome," said Judith. "Though we didn't have to walk back to the hotel today, thank goodness."

"What happened?" asked Ciara.

"We were walking along slowly, exhausted by the heat, not to mention stuffing ourselves silly with culture, you know, art, religion and history," said Nuala, "when Saint Felix came galloping along. He took in the situation at a glance and sent us back to the hotel in a fleet of taxis."

"Come off it, Nuala, there is no St Felix, you're having us on again," said Gráinne scathingly.

"She isn't for once," said Judith. "It's all true, except she forgot to mention that he paid for the taxis too."

"I can't believe it," said the unconvinced Gráinne.

"He is really Felix Costello, a friend of Miss Ryan's," Monica informed her earnestly. "But don't tell anyone. We don't want Miss Grimes to find out."

"Why on earth: Miss Ryan is a teacher, she can have a boyfriend in Rome, can't she?" said Gráinne. "Though I suppose Miss Grimes wouldn't approve. Is it true that she goes around checking that you are in your beds every night?"

"She did last night," said Aileen. "Perhaps we should hide behind the door when she comes in tonight and give her a shock."

"You could jump out and ask her one of your

crossword puzzles," said Deirdre. "That would send her out screaming fast enough."

"That reminds me," said Aileen, producing the dreaded puzzle in its plastic cover. "Here's one for you to try. 'Any of the cavities in the cranial boxes', it could begin with an S and it's five letters."

"Give it a rest, Aileen," begged Josie. "You'll ruin our evening."

"Keep your hair on. I thought you'd agreed to help," said Aileen inured to insult. "What about a Spanish family associated with Italy? She looked around hopefully.

"The first one, could it be 'sinus'?" asked Ciara, who quite liked crosswords.

"It fits, great, I'll write it in. Thanks, Ciara, that's only sixteen now," said Aileen in a pleased voice.

"We got some fab T-shirts today, at the steps," Fidelma told the visitors. "Only £2.50 a pair!"

"Would you like to see ours?" asked Eithne. "I have to go to my room anyway and I'll bring those postcards of yours back with me, Nuala. I won't be a minute."

"Do you realise that we leave for our day trip to Naples at seven tomorrow morning," said Gwendoline, when Eithne had left the room.

"I know, but getting up in the morning here is much easier than at home," said Gráinne. "It's the sun, I suppose."

"We have to take in Pompeii too, everyone says it's well worth going to see," said Josie. "I'm sorry we can't go to Capri though, I'd like a sea voyage."

The door opened and Eithne bounced in wearing a smart navy blue suede jacket. She threw a packet of postcards over to Nuala, then twirled around as much as she could in such a confined space. "What do you think, girls? Isn't it super?" she called cheerfully, posing like a model.

"Is that the jacket Miss Ryan was given?" asked Gráinne, impressed. "It's really cool, isn't it?"

"It is indeed. I hope she doesn't catch Eithne wearing it," said Aileen.

"Don't fuss, Aileen," said Eithne. "I only wanted to show it to Ciara and Gráinne. I'm going now." She turned and made for the door.

"Don't be long," warned Nuala. "Miss Ryan lent us her mini electric kettle, it's plugged in now and soon we'll be able to have some coffee and biscuits."

"The only trouble is, we'll have to take it in turns," explained Judith, producing a packet of powdered milk, "as we've only four mugs between us!"

8

A Wanted Wallet

Eithne didn't delay. She ran down to the room which she shared with Fidelma, Monica and Gwendoline. In her haste, she did not even notice Enrico, who was hovering around in the corridor. Once in the room, she quickly divested herself of the precious jacket. Then she folded it carefully so that it looked as if it had never been touched. Slipping it into the *Luichi* bag, she replaced it at the bottom of her empty suitcase. Then she ran lightly back to rejoin her friends, and soon was enjoying coffee and almond biscuits with them.

Enrico, standing outside Eithne's room, couldn't believe his luck. He waited for a few minutes, then slipped quietly into the room, where he soon found the navy blue jacket. Giula, who had followed him, waited around the corner. When Enrico came out of the room minutes later, he found her there waiting for him. "Hand them over," she ordered crisply.

He looked sadly at her. "Hand over what, Giula, I don't understand," he said in his quiet voice.

"You do understand, a film strip of five

negatives which you stole from Roberto's safe."

He was about to protest his innocence when he noticed the small automatic revolver in her hand. "Are you working for Roberto?" he asked sulkily. "Because if you are, I have bad news for him. The negatives are not in the coat any more."

"I don't believe you," she said coldly, still pointing the gun at him.

"It's true all the same. I had them in a leather wallet and when you disturbed me yesterday, I slipped it in one of the pockets of the jacket. Well, I have searched the jacket. It's in that room there lying in an empty suitcase, but the wallet with the negatives in it is gone," he replied dejectedly.

"There is no trace of it? Those girls must have taken them." Giula looked at him. "What would girls, foreigners like them, want with the negatives?" she asked scornfully. "They couldn't possibly understand their significance."

Enrico turned his sad eyes on her. "They probably found the wallet and thought it was pretty with the two white birds on it. The leather is good too, I got it from an *Americano* only last year."

She gave a low laugh. "The same way you got the negatives from Roberto's safe, I suppose. How did you find out about them, anyway?"

"It was quite by accident," he said simply. "I overheard him talking on the phone one day to someone. He said he would want one hundred thousand dollars for them. I thought I could give up singing stupid songs to tourists every night if I had even half that money, so I decided to remove them from his safe. Roberto is rich. I needed the money more than him."

She laughed grimly. "What do you think he will do to you if I tell him that you took them from his safe?" she asked.

"You can't prove a thing," he pointed out. "But if you were to join with me and forget about Roberto we could find the negatives, they can't be far away, and make the money for ourselves."

Giula thought for a minute before deciding. "Right, we'll do it together. Who cares about Roberto anyway or the Contessa? We'd better leave here soon, we might be seen. Shouldn't you be at work?" she asked.

"*Si*, in half an hour. Meet me at *San Patricios*, the Irish bar at 22:00, nobody knows me there, and we can work it out."

She waved him on with the gun. "You go to work," she said. "If you are telling the truth, you've nothing to worry about, we'll make that hundred thousand I have the contacts. If not, watch out, I'm a ruthless person."

He said nothing more, just melted quietly away.

Nuala didn't come across the missing wallet until Ciara and Gráinne had gone back to their own hotel and the others to their room. "Look what I've found," she said to Aileen who was getting ready for bed. "Pretty, isn't it? I wonder where it came from." She opened the wallet, taking out the strip of negatives and holding it up

to the light. "They are all the same," she said
slowly. "It looks like two men and two women I
think, but of course they mean nothing to me."

She passed it over to Aileen who confirmed
that the negatives were of two unknown men and
women. As she passed them back to Nuala, Josie
came in all excitement.

"Do you remember the singing guy in that
place last night? Well, I saw him hanging around
here earlier this evening!" she said.

"What was he doing here?" asked Judith,
coming in from the bathroom.

"I don't know, but Miss Grimes is now on her
way down to the manager. She said the singer had
come up to her room earlier this afternoon,
looking for Miss Ryan, with some story about the
suede jacket. She sent him packing, of course.
What do you think of that?"

Nuala looked at Josie, then at the negatives in
her hand, then back at Josie again. "I wonder,"
she said at last. "I wonder could these have come
from that navy blue suede jacket. I'll have to ask
Eithne."

She left the room, returning with Eithne who
was all agog to hear about the singing guy and the
wallet which had turned up unexpectedly on
Nuala's table. She held up the negatives to the
light, but like Aileen and Nuala before her, all she
could make out was the two couples in each
negative.

"Reconstruct the events leading up to the
discovery by Nuala of the wallet with the birds on

71

it," ordered Aileen, who rather liked detective novels.

Eithne laughed but obediently started. "I put on the jacket and put the postcards in one of the pockets before leaving my room. When I came in here I took the postcards out of the pocket, placing them on Nuala's bedside table there."

"It looks as if the wallet was in the pocket too," said Nuala. "Eithne was so interested in showing us the jacket that she never noticed that the postcards had got mixed up with it."

"It's a blooming mystery, that's what it is," said Josie. "Do you think that they belong to the singing guy from *La Grotta Azzuria*?"

"I can't see why he didn't say so to Miss Grimes then," said Eithne. "Anyway, I'd better go back and tell the story to the others."

"These postcards are really good," said Judith, who hadn't been paying much attention to the conversation around her. She had been totally absorbed in looking at Nuala's postcards.

"What are they of?" asked Josie, holding out her hand for one.

"They are really only photographs of the famous pictures we saw in that church of *Santa Maria del Popolo*, you know Caravaggio and Pinturicchio," said Nuala.

"This is the Crucifixion of St Peter and that's the Conversion of St Paul," said Judith, handing them over to Josie. "You couldn't take photographs as good as that yourself, especially as that corner in the church was so dark."

"Gwendoline certainly tried," said Aileen. "She's taken a photograph of everything we've stopped at, including loads of Monica and Miss Ryan."

"You can have any of those you like, Judith," said Nuala. "I know how much these famous pictures mean to you."

"Thanks, Nuala, you're a pal. Miss Ryan was telling me that we have to see the Basilica of St John Lateran, there's a restored fresco in it by Giotto which was painted in 1300 for the first Holy Year. Imagine seven hundred years old!" said Judith in an awestruck voice.

"You know," complained Aileen, getting into her bed. "This room is turning into an art school but if I were to ask one of you the name of a famous artist, three and four letter words with a 'G' in the second word, you'd all screech and say 'oh no Aileen, not now'."

"Is it one of your puzzles?" asked Judith in an amused voice.

"As it happens," replied Aileen in a dignified voice, "it isn't. I just made it up myself. It was Van Gogh. I know about artists too, but I don't want to spend my whole evening talking about them."

"What do you think of our mysterious wallet with the two white birds and its contents?" asked Nuala.

"Well, if you really want my advice, I'd take out that strip of film and put another one in its place. Leave it here tomorrow and see what happens when we are away on the trip to Naples."

"That's a good idea, Aileen," said Nuala, rooting around among her belongings and producing a few strips of film. For some reason she wasn't satisfied. Then she ran out of the room saying something about Gwendoline.

"She'd better be quick," said Aileen lying back against her pillows. "The *Cleaner* will be around soon, checking that we're not having a good time laughing at something."

Nuala returned shortly afterwards looking pleased. "As I thought, Gwendoline has stacks of negatives and I found some with two couples in them that would pass for the originals. They were taken at some party of her mother's and she can't remember who the people are."

"Where will you put them?" asked Josie, messing with her hair as usual. "How would you like my hair in a plait?"

"I'd love it," replied Nuala absently. "I think the best thing is to put Gwendoline's film in the wallet, like so, and then put the pretty thing in the second drawer under my socks and shirts."

"Yes, that's better than leaving it lying around. If it's gone from the drawer, we'll know that it was deliberately taken," said Aileen approvingly.

"Would he have the neck to come back again tomorrow?" asked Judith.

"He might have an accomplice, of course," said Josie. "Wouldn't you love to know what's so important about the negatives too?"

"I wonder how they got into the suede jacket as well," said Nuala. "Anyway, they're going into my money belt now and that will be around my slim form all day tomorrow."

There was a knock on the bedroom door. Josie ran over, opened it slightly and peered out. Miss Grimes came into the room. "Everyone in bed? Good. You look very flushed, Nuala. I hope this dreadful heat isn't too much for you. Go to sleep now, we have a very early start in the morning."

"Good night, Miss Grimes," they chorused. As she was about to leave she said to Josie, politely holding the door open for her. "I have spoken to the manager. He says that no one answering to my description of that man has any business to be in this hotel. He is investigating the matter. Lock your door after I've gone, goodnight girls."

She left the room. As soon as Josie had locked the door Nuala got out of bed. "Phew, that was a rush," she said. "I'd better wash now." She went into the tiny bathroom and closed the door behind her.

In the fifth years' bedroom Sharon Kennedy stood at the window, looking gloomily out at the street far below them. "Look at them," she said. "Crowds of people all talking and laughing as they go out for a bit of crack. There's an Irish bar only around the corner and I bet they'll all be going there."

Her great friend Lisa Shevlin joined her at the window handing her a piece of paper which looked like a brochure of some kind. "The guy at the desk gave me this, he says the night tour of

Rome is worth going on. It says here that it starts at 10 p.m. and lasts about three hours. What do you think? Apparently they pick you up at the hotel too."

Sharon looked at the brochure and brightened up. "It has possibilities, especially as we won't have old Grimes with us, that woman gives me a pain. You never know who we might meet."

"Does it leave us back here too?" asked Nessa, another of the fifth years in the room with them.

"It does, it's better than doing nothing," said Sharon. "I never thought this tour would be so dull, just going from one ancient place to another."

"The best time would be tomorrow night. We can say that we are so tired from spending hours at Pompeii, that we are going to bed early, then slip out when the coach arrives for us," said Lisa, who was really keen to see Rome by night.

"We can book our tour before we leave for Naples tomorrow," said Sharon.

San Patricios was full as usual. Giulia pushed her way through the noisy crowd, who were shouting, laughing and even singing as they downed a variety of drinks from different countries, especially Ireland. When she spied Enrico, he was sitting alone at the very back of the room. "Ciao," she said dropping into a seat beside him. He seemed pleased to see her. She got straight down to business. "I've fixed it up so that I can search the hotel tomorrow. You'd better keep out of

76

sight. If I find it, I will let you know at once. Then I'll meet my contact and see how much she is prepared to pay."

"What about Roberto? he will expect you in to work as usual."

She laughed. "Roberto thinks I am off to *Firenze* tonight on a visit to my mother. If I have to ring you at work I will say I am your sister Domenica, right?"

He smiled and lifted his glass. "Right, to success and to many million lira."

9

Tours and Theft

They were all finished breakfast and waiting for the coach when it arrived on the following morning punctually at seven a.m. Nuala and Aileen made a final check of the leather wallet and its contents, replacing it under the socks in the second drawer of the dressing-table, before running downstairs again and joining the others.

"It's extraordinary how cheerful everyone is so early in the morning," Eithne said to Judith as they were boarding the coach.

"It's so much easier to get up early here than at home. I suppose it's the lovely summer weather," replied Judith. "I'm really looking forward to this trip, aren't you?"

"I suppose so, it's going to be a long one though, thirteen hours. I hope we won't be sick of sitting in the coach for so long," replied Eithne.

In the seat behind them Aileen settled herself comfortably, extracting a thick copybook and pen from the bag on her knee.

"What are they for?" asked Nuala, from the seat beside her.

"This is my Rome journal. It's such a bore

writing it up every night, I had this brilliant idea: I would write as we go along today, listen to the guide and then write down what he says," retorted Aileen, looking particularly pleased with herself.

"It will be a nice change from that awful crossword, anyway," said Nuala thankfully.

"Ha, that's what you think," said Aileen. "I have it here and we can do a few as we go along. You're the clever one, Nuala."

"I cerainly am, well cuss my mouth for bringing up the subject," replied Nuala with a groan.

As soon as they had crossed the city, the guide could be heard over the intercom "We leave Rome in a southerly direction," he was saying, "taking the highway of the sun which will bring us across the fertile Latium countryside."

Everyone stopped talking to look out their windows, trying to look intelligent and interested. Nuala watched Aileen diligently write in her journal every time the guide spoke. About halfway to Naples, when they had just passed the famous Abbey of Monte Cassino, curiosity got the better of Nuala and she leaned over to see how much Aileen had managed to get in.

After a mad dash across the ancient city of Rome, Nuala read in Aileen's clear handwriting, *the Irish pilgrims from St Brigid's on the Boyne were taken along the highway of the sun, whatever that means, surrounded by millions of crazy motorists and touring coaches who were travelling as fast as*

*if they were competing in the Grand Prix or else
being chased by devils out of Hell. Fortunately, the
Irish pilgrims were travelling in an air-conditioned
coach or else they would have been suffocated by
clouds of carbon monoxide, bringing grief to at
least forty-five Irish homes. As the pilgrims
listened politely to their guide, they looked out of
the windows to see the promised sights of Roman
castles, vineyards, fields of grain and vegetables,
only to have the view obscured for them by the
same maniacal motor-cars and buses rushing
along beside them, full perhaps of pilgrims from
other lands trying to see the sights too.*

"Aileen, you idiot, you can't give that up to Miss
Ryan," laughed Nuala.

"Why not, it's the truth, isn't it?" replied
Aileen briskly. "Now, what about a word or two
before he starts boring on again."

"All right, let's get it over with then," replied
Nuala in a resigned voice.

"'Affecting an oily charm,' eight letters?"
Aileen, said looking hopefully at Nuala, who
shrugged and said, "Try another."

"'Decorative delicate fabric woven in an open
web', four letters, on of which is C. I know what,
it could only be lace," said Aileen triumphantly.
"That's only 16 left now."

The rest of the journey passed surprisingly
quickly. In no time at all they were travelling
along the modern ring-road that seemed
suspended around the city of Naples, with

everyone exclaiming at the marvellous view they now had of the distant hills and blue sea. They were glad all the same to get out of the coach and stretch their legs. They were then taken on a short tour of the Royal Palace, the Basilica of St Francesco di Paola, the Opera House and the Gallery of Umberto I. After that, to the great relief of the majority of the girls, they were taken to a restaurant overlooking the famous Bay of Naples.

They all crowded happily into the restaurant looking forward eargerly to what the guide had promised them was the most famous Neapolitan dish in the world. Soon a plate of steaming hot food was placed in front of each "Irish pilgrim" to borrow Aileen's nomenclature. "Why," exclaimed a very surprised, though relieved, Monica, "it's pizza. I thought it was going to be some weird food. I love pizza!"

"This is the nicest pizza I've ever eaten," said Josie. "The base is thin and light and the sauce out of this world."

"The cheese has a yummy flavour too," said Eithne.

"It's Mozzarella cheese," said Judith. "That's why it looks so white and creamy."

Everyone munching happily away nodded in agreement. "Anything would taste good after our mini breakfast at 6.30 a.m.," said Aileen, who didn't believe in going overboard about anything in Italy.

"I would have liked to have gone to Capri," said Josie as they were finishing their lunch with fruit and little amaretti biscuits.

"Yes, it's a pity we're missing the Blue Grotto," agreed Fidelma, "but Miss O'Brien says everyone raves over Pompeii and there's no way we can visit both places in one day."

"It's a shame on a hot day like this to miss the chance of a cruise to Capri, with gentle sea breezes blowing over us," said Eithne soulfully.

"And Nuala singing, you know the song they use in that ice cream ad, as we lie back relaxing on the deck," said Aileen, grinning.

"You mean just one gelato," said Josie. "Now that would have been brilliant."

"What we need is Keaney baby," said Nuala ignoring the talk about her singing for them. "If she was here, we would have all the music you could want."

A chorus of laughing agreement came from the rest of the girls, who remembered with affection their former games teacher Gretta Keane, who had been apt to sit down and play the piano whenever the mood took her, which was often, and also her habit of wearing fur-lined boots all the year round. She had left the school about a year previously and had married an Italian, hence Nuala bringing her to their attention now.

"I'm surprised we haven't met her in Rome," said Aileen.

"Miss O'Brien told us that it was all arranged to meet her but it fell through at the last minute for some reason or other," said Gráinne.

"That's a terrible pity," said Nuala.

"I was really anxious to check up on her foot gear."

"She'd hardly wear those furlined boots in this heat," said Aileen. "Though nothing would surprise me where Miss Keane, or should I call her Signora Fioretti, is concerned."

It was time to leave Miss Ryan advised them to buy some bottles of water as they would be two hours wandering round the excavations in Pompeii.

About the same time as the St Brigid's coach was speeding along to the city ruined by the volcano in 79 AD, a woman dressed neatly in a navy overall was entering the room Gwendoline and her friends were occupying in the hotel on the Esquiline Hill. Swiftly she opened drawers and presses and expertly searched them. Fifteen minutes later, she was searching the adjacent rooms. Eventually, and just as she was about to give up hope, she opened the second drawer of Nuala's dressing-table. She left the hotel very soon afterwards.

The first thing the contingent from St Brigid's noticed when they arrived in Pompeii was the heat. It rose up in waves as they walked along the straight streets between the ruined houses.

"Imagine this whole place was once covered by thirty feet of ash," said Nuala to Aileen as they reached the amphitheatre and sat down on one of its tiered seats.

"Whoever cleared it away did a brilliant job," said Aileen, looking around her. "In fact, the pavements here are in better condition than the ones in Rome."

"Hi, Nuala, come over here," called Judith, standing at one of the entrances. "And you too, Aileen. I want to take a photo of you in this huge entrance here. If you look you can see it frames Vesuvius, looking blue and innocent in the background."

When Judith had taken several photographs, they were joined by Josie, who wanted to show them the decorations still visible on the inner walls of some of the houses there. "I've taken more photos here than anywhere else," she said. "The light is so good. I'm hoping for brilliant results."

Aileen took a swig from her water bottle. "I'm so hot," she said. "I wonder would it be any cooler anywhere else."

"There was some talk of going over to see the crater on Mount Vesuvius," said Judith. "Let's find Miss Ryan and see if that's still on."

Miss Ryan was sitting resting from the heat and talking to the other teachers when they found her.

"I'm sorry," she said. "The crater is too far away for us to go and see in the short time left. Have you visited the *Casa di Menando*?"

They shook their heads so she good naturedly took them off to see the largest and most intact house in the ruined city. They went in through the entrance where Miss Ryan showed them the atrium in which the pool was once used to catch rain water from an opening in the ceiling. The last thing they looked at before they left was a fresco depicting the Trojan War which was painted on one of the walls. As the teacher pointed out some of the features of this fresco, explaining their significance, Josie, getting bored, wickedly whispered to Aileen, "Just look at Judith, she's goggling at that picture like a stunned mullet."

In an effort to control the giggles threatening to overcome her, Aileen moved backwards and knocked into Monica. She, taken unawares, nearly tripped over Gwendoline, who staggered about drunkenly.

"I think we'd better leave," said Miss Ryan, "before we knock over the remains of this house which has managed to survive a volcano and centuries of being buried in ash before we arrived.'

When they got to the coach some time later, the general comment was that Pompeii had been great but the terrible heat had spoiled it a bit for them.

"I told you," said Eithne, as they drove away, "we would have been much better off sailing to Capri and seeing the Blue Grotto there. But would anyone listen to me?"

"Frankly, no," said Josie. "As if we are ever asked what we would like to do, you silly goop."

Miles away in Rome, Giulia crossed the *Piazzo del Popolo* and sat down at a table outside a café there. Enrico, who was toying with a cup of coffee, barely acknowledged her arrival.

"Here's your share," she said, slipping an envelope across the table to him. "5,000 dollars as promised."

His sad eyes lit up for once, especially when he had checked the contents of the brown envelope. "How did you get it?" he asked eagerly.

"As I told you on the phone," she replied. "I found your wallet with the white birds on it under some clothes in a drawer in one of the rooms in the hotel. The negatives were in it. I took them to my contact saying $10,000 down and $40,000 when they were developed. She didn't even haggle. I have to go back later. I'll meet you in *San Patricio*'s at twenty-two hours, same seat."

Then she left. He watched her until she passed out of sight in the crowds, then he too got up and walked away in another direction.

It was nearly 8 p.m. before the coach arrived at the hotel in Rome again as the whole party had been taken to a restaurant for their evening meal on their way back. However, Nuala, Aileen, Judith and Josie hadn't forgotten about the negatives in the wallet. As soon as they reached their room Nuala ran over and opened the second drawer of the dressing-table. Pushing her socks aside, she looked then she tipped out the contents of the drawer on the floor. "It's gone!" she announced. "It's really gone. I can't believe it! I wonder who took it?"

"We'll never know now," said Judith.

"What makes you think that?" said Aileen. "Remember the real negatives weren't in the wallet. Nuala still has them."

"Of course, I forgot that. Do you think that it was the singing guy then?" asked Judith.

"I don't know, whoever took it must have searched all our rooms," said Nuala.

"I know," said Josie. "Let's report it to Miss Grimes so that she can make life hell for the manager. First of all check that nothing else is missing."

A thorough search of the room revealed that nothing else was missing; in fact it was hard to believe that the wallet could have been taken, only that it was missing. Josie and Nuala went off to report the theft to Miss Grimes, while Aileen and Judith went to warn the rest of the group not to mention anything about the missing wallet to Miss Ryan.

10

Black Business at the Basilica

The interview with the manager wasn't quite as satisfactory as the justly incensed Miss Grimes had expected. While he sympathised with her problem it soon became obvious that he didn't take her story seriously. A mystery thief, who had not disturbed anything and who only stole a leather wallet of no great value, was something impossible to understand. Perhaps, he gently insinuated, the young ladies had made a mistake. It would have been very easy to have lost this wallet sightseeing in Naples or even Pompeii.

"Very well," the teacher said. "But I'm not satisfied at all. Remember, I spoke to that man myself."

As she returned to her room, she reflected how different it had been when she had been in Rome on a previous occasion many years before. One day, as she and a friend had been travelling to the Vatican on the bus, someone had stolen her friend's purse. The driver had reacted instantly to the complaint, locking the bus door and driving it to the nearest police station. There the bus had been searched, the purse found (empty of course) and six people had been questioned and taken away. All very satisfactory even though her friend had never recovered her money. Reaching her bedroom, she was surprised to find Vanessa already in bed, reading up about St Paul's Basilica where she intended taking the girls the following day.

"I know it's not very late but I'm exhausted," explained Vanessa. "Most of the girls are asleep. I've checked them for you."

"Thank goodness. That was very thoughtful of you," said Dottie. "I'm strangely tired myself. It has been a very long day."

Twenty-five minutes later the night porter went into the hotel lounge where Sharon Kennedy was entertaining the other fifth years. "The coach is here," he informed her, "to take you to the 'Rome by Night' office."

"Thank you, Pietro," she said. Finishing her drink, she got up. "Come on girls, let's go. We'll be back around midnight, I suppose.'

About half a mile away from the hotel Giulia was standing in the Contessa's salon looking bad-tempered and grim. She had arrived to collect the balance of her payment for the negatives, only to be met by the bad news that they weren't the right ones after all.

"Giulia," said the Contessa in a cold voice. "I am not pleased with you. Only I have had satisfactory work from you before, I would say you were trying to double-cross me." She spread out some photographs on the table before Giulia. "Who are these people?" she asked snappily.

Giulia looked down at the stylishly dressed couples in front of her. "I don't know," she stammered, which wasn't surprising as they were photographs of some friends of Gwendoline's family that had been taken at one of the O'Hagan parties. Enrico must have lied, was her first furious reaction; I'll get him for this.

"You said you were tipped off about them being in a tourist's room in a hotel near here," said the Contessa. "You'd better get the right negatives very soon or else there will be big trouble for you. Remember we've paid you 10,000 dollars already."

Giulia paced up and down the salon. "Why did they switch the negatives?" she said at last. "There was no way they could have known anything. I'll go now."

Snatching up the wallet she almost ran out of the salon in her eagerness to meet Enrico and confront him, leaving the Contessa sitting immobile in the silent room, looking very thoughtful.

The shrill sound of the telephone ringing broke her reverie. Picking it up she said *"Villa Mercedes"* in her usual manner.

"Contessa," said a familiar voice. "Desirée here. Have you managed to collect those five items yet?"

"I have not. Do you take me for a magician?" snapped the Contessa, who didn't want to admit to Desirée that she had handed out good money for nothing.

"Kindly get on with it. It's very important to me. I've just been made chairperson of one of those committees set up by the EU to regulate the size and number of ancient monuments per square hectare. It's a very prestigious position and I wouldn't want anything to go wrong."

"It's very important to you, is it? What about me? What do I get out of it? I don't know about this special envoy business, it's having a bad effect on you."

"Please don't be so foolish, Contessa. I think I'd better join you in Rome. Expect me tomorrow evening. We'll need to talk. Goodbye until then."

The Contessa slammed down the phone, frowning at the wall in front of her, where a stout gentleman looked down at her in a very superior way from his gilded frame. "You're right, Grandpapa," she said in a nasty voice. "Giulia is not to be trusted any more, she needs watching."

The following morning was hot and fair like all the other days that week, something the girls were still finding a pleasant surprise. "I think we are so lucky to be staying in our little hotel," said Josie, as they took their places in the underground train, which was taking them quite near to the Basilica of St Paul Without the Walls.

"Why?" asked Eithne. "I know it's all right, but why specially?"

"Well," said Josie. "The main bunch in that other hotel are taken everywhere by coach. It's much better fun to go around the way Miss Ryan takes us. I've never been on an underground before, for instance."

"I agree," said Judith. "When we look back on this tour, our memories won't be only of the famous touristy places but little things too. The fruit markets, the shops, even that nice old lady in the ice cream shop who was so friendly to us."

"You sound like an old granny yourself, Judith," said Aileen. "All this concentration on old paintings is affecting you badly."

"There's no need to act like something mean beginning with C, three letters, is there, Aileen?" said Fidelma, defending her cousin.

"No, Fidelma," said Nuala. "Don't, you'll only start her off again."

"You nedn't worry," said Aileen, not put out in the least by Fidelma's stricture. "I've only about ten left, which I'm more than capable of solving myself."

"Have you actually worked out the aristrocratic title that originally meant companion?" asked Nuala. "What was it?"

"That's one of the ten I've yet to do, but I'll get it, don't worry," was Aileen's calm reply.

"That reminds me," said Eithne. "We forgot to tell them, Fidelma, about the fifth years. They slipped out of the hotel last night and went on a night tour of Rome, until about 1 a.m!"

"You're not serious," said Josie. "I don't believe you."

"Shush," said Eithne, lowering her voice. "Fidelma and myself were still eating what they call breakfast here, when Nessa Jones and Nellie Quinn came in all giggles and excitement. It appears that the five of them had been picked up last night by a minibus, which took them to the tour office. According to Nessa, Rome was brilliant by night and who did they meet but Gertie Kelly and Mary Lamb."

"Not *the* Gertie and Lambsie," said Aileen referring to two past pupils of St Brigid's, who had left the school only about a year before this and were last heard of training to be secretaries.

"The very ones," said Eithne. "They are now working in Rome and apparently if Gertie had only known that we were coming here, she would have shown Sharon and Co a few really hot nightspots and even introduced them to a few guys.'

"I bet Lambsie agreed with her too," said Fidelma.

"Those two were always guy-crazy. Do you remember, Eithne, the time they brought us around Drogheda, we nearly went ape following them from boutique to boutique looking for something to wear to the Newgrange school social."

"I never knew you two were friendly with Nessa," said Nuala.

"We're not really, but Nessa lives near us at home. Anyway, they were dying to tell someone about their adventures."

"I don't suppose Miss Grimes was with them," grinned Josie. "They'd better watch it all the same.

Remember that form all our parents had to sign about not drinking alcohol or nipping out at night without permission."

"We think they've planned something for tonight too, judging by the whispering that went on between them when the others turned up for breakfast later on," said Eithne.

"How did Miss Grimes not miss them?" asked Nuala. "And she's supposed to be so suspicious too.'

"The story is that she was so tired after Pompeii that she just went to bed as soon as we got back," said Eithne, who was one of those people who always knew the gossip wherever they were.

They hadn't very far to walk and soon were passing through wonderfully decorated doors and into a wide passage, which led into the Basilica proper. "It's vast, isn't it?" said Josie, looking wide-eyed around her.

Miss Ryan smiled and quietly replied, "It's the second biggest in Rome, only St Peter's is bigger."

The place was full of people, the great majority of whom were winding around the Basilica on conducted tours. Miss Ryan and her group, falling in behind the crowds, soon reached the Papal altar. Only the Pope is allowed to say Mass there, situated, as it is above the burial place of St Paul himself. Then they visited the many side chapels full of statues, precious mosaics and a wonderful crucifix dating from the beginning of the 14th century.

"It's really hard to take it all in," said Judith.

Miss Ryan stopped and pointed out a sixteen-foot high intricately carved candelabrum which towered high above them. "This marvellous candle-holder dates from the end of the 12th century, about the same time as the Normans invaded Ireland," she said. "It was made to hold the paschal-candle, you know, the one that they light at Easter."

"How do you know so much about Rome and places like here?" asked Deirdre, as they all looked with respect at the ancient artefact, vainly trying to imagine what scenes it must have witnessed during its eight-hundred-year span.

Miss Ryan laughed. "I'm supposed to be a history teacher," she said. "And your parents have paid a lot of money for this tour. I would like you to get good value from it as well."

After an hour or two wandering around St Paul's the group found themselves in the cloisters which enclosed an oasis of a garden. Four large formal beds edged with roses and enclosed by clipped green hedges, with paths running around them and a fountain in the middle, met their pleased gaze.

"Let's sit down and rest for a while," said the teacher. "It's been a wonderful experience, but a short rest will be good for all of us.'

"The heat is getting to you," said Gwendoline. "It's a pity we have to wear jeans instead of shorts."

"You'd have to change while visiting churches, it wouldn't be worth it," replied Miss Ryan.

It was quiet and peaceful in the garden as very few people seemed to visit it. They all sat down on stone seats beside one of the flower-beds.

Then Gwendoline, asking Nuala to hold a large holdall for her, produced from its innards a thick bundle of newly developed photographs which she proudly handed around. Aileen, at the edge of the group gazed idly at the passers-by, while waiting her turn for the photos. She noticed a slim dark-haired woman looking curiously over at the third years, who were laughing merrily. Gwendoline was an erratic, if dedicated, photographer and had produced some hilarious shots, a notable one being of the famous statue of Moses, minus his head.

"This one would have been brilliant if only you had kept your hand steady," Monica was saying about a slightly fuzzy view of Mount Vesuvius, when Aileen saw the woman rooting around in her handbag and dropping something on the ground.

"Hey," called Aileen. "You've dropped something!"

Seemingly the woman didn't hear her as she just walked on, turning the corner of the flower-bed. Aileen ran over and picked up the dropped object. "Why," she said as Nuala and Judith joined her. "It's a leather wallet and it's the image of the other one with the two white birds on it."

"They're probably two a penny in Rome," said Nuala, "but we had better hurry if we're going to catch up with her to return it."

The three of them ran along the path, reaching the woman as she was turning towards the exit. "Excuse me, you dropped this," said Aileen, breathlessly as she thrust the wallet at her and hoped the woman understood English.

Apparently she did, for taking the wallet, she said in a heavily accented but friendly voice, "Thank you. I wouldn't like to lose this. I've never seen another one like it anywhere. It's so pretty, isn't it?"

Aileen stared, then said in a surprised voice, "That's funny, we, that is, my friend, lost one like this only yesterday."

The woman smiled sympathetically. "I'm so sorry. I hope nothing of value was in it."

Then to her companions' astonishment, Nuala said in an odd dreamy voice, "There's no need to be sorry, our relationship was a brief, here today, gone tomorrow, type of one. The pretty wallet with the two white birds on it just appeared on my bedside table like magic and the following day it disappeared just as mysteriously as it came. This time from a drawer in my dressing-table."

The woman, looking slightly confused, asked in a carefully casual voice, "Was there anything in the wallet, did you look?"

"I looked in it all right. Nothing much was there only a bit of film, a strip of negative I believe. What did we do with them, Aileen?"

Aileen looked blank then, noticing Gwendoline's bulging holdall, said desperately, "I don't really remember, perhaps it got mixed up in that bag of yours there."

"Of course," said Nuala, unzipping the bag and taking out about a dozen envelopes all containing negatives. She handed them to Aileen with a smile. "Perhaps we put it in one of these."

Then for the next five minutes, Nuala, Aileen and even Judith solemnly looked through the envelopes and examined the negatives. "No," said Nuala at last. "It's not there, such a pity, you might have been able to tell us who the people in it were and now we'll never know."

"Why me?" said the woman in a bad-tempered voice. "I don't know what you mean."

"Well," said Nuala. "You seem to have the mysterious wallet, I just thought you might know something about the negatives."

The woman's face darkened, then she said in an expressionless voice, "I don't know what your game is but if you find those negatives, which are mine, keep them safe. I will be in touch again and remember it might be to your advantage if you return them."

Then she turned and walked smartly away, unaware that she was being watched from behind one of the many twisted columns which formed part of the cloisters there. "The double-crossing fiend, it's obvious she's bargaining with them, whoever they are," muttered the onlooker who was swathed in a long black scarf. "Damn this scarf on my face, I can't make out a thing with it."

By the time she had unwrapped herself and looked out at the garden again, the only people she could see were two elderly ladies walking along a path, looking at the rather tired roses.

Later on when the girls were walking back to the station, Josie, who had been in front with Miss Ryan, came back to where Nuala and Aileen were taking up the rear. "Nuala," she said. "You know that woman you were talking to in St Paul's. Well I've just seen her getting into a car and driving off with a man, who looked very like that singer with the sad eyes. You know, the one I saw hanging around our rooms in the hotel the other night."

"I'm not really surprised," said Nuala. "It's obvious they are a pair of crooks."

11

Nicked Negatives

The train journey back from St Paul's was agony
for Aileen and Judith, who were dying to discuss
their encounter with the woman in the garden,
especially Nuala's surprising behaviour during it.
In consequence while their minds were actively
wrestling with the mystery of the wallet, their
contribution to the conversation going on around
them was almost non-existent, so much so that
even Miss Ryan noticed it.

"They must be tired from the heat and all the
walking around the Basilica," she said in her
kindly way to the other girls, as they walked from
the station to the hotel.

However, all was changed the minute they
reached their bedroom. "Now, Nuala," said Judith,
pushing her into a chair. "Explain yourself at
once. Why did you tell all to that woman,
spinning her such a yarn?"

Nuala lay back and laughed. "It was so funny.
If you could only have seen your faces, talk about
stunned mullets!"

"I think we were brilliant," said Aileen.
"Throwing that question at me about the
negatives too. What's it all about, Nuala?"

"Use your heads. Did you ever see anything as obvious at dropping that wallet on the ground in front of us? It wouldn't have fooled a child."

"It fooled me," said Judith. "It never even crossed my mind that she wasn't genuine."

"Last night when Josie came in and told us that the singing guy was prowling around outside our room, it came to me in a flash that he had been near our table when I was telling Gráinne the story about the jackets," said Nuala. "Don't you remember how noisy that place was and how we had to shout to be heard?"

"That's true, Nuala," said Aileen. "I remember him holding his bowl and looking sad, just behind our table."

Josie came into the room then, so Aileen gave her a quick version of the encounter in the garden. "Wow!" said Josie. "What do you think they are up to?"

Nuala took the negatives out of her belt and held them up to the light. "See that round black spot behind that man's head," she said as the others crowded around looking at the negatives. "Don't touch it, but the film is much thicker there and I believe it's what they call a microdot, proving that those two are industrial spies."

"Industrial spies! What do they do?" asked Aileen.

"Say you owned a detergent factory and had a bright chemist working for you who invented a better product than any of your rivals. The word gets around about it, this is where the spy comes in. He or she infiltrates the lab and with a special camera photographs the formula, etc. so small that it fits into that round circle. They sell this information for thousands."

"How do they use the dot?" asked Judith.

"I think they have special magnifying lens which will bring it up to whatever size they want. I've just read a brilliant book about a woman detective who foils a gang of spies who are out to wreck a computer firm."

"Shouldn't we go to the police with this information, then?" asked Judith.

"Come on Judith, with my Italian and their English, how could I tell them about it – in sign language? Besides, we're foreigners, they wouldn't believe us," said Nuala.

"Is that why you told her so much?" asked Josie. "So that they would know you've guessed their game? I'm not complaining, I like our adventures, but do you think it's wise or safe?"

"Well, I thought it might be interesting to see what they do next," said Nuala. "As for danger, there's a whole crowd of us here and we'll be going back to Ireland in a couple of days anyway, so I'm not worried."

Aileen laughed. "You're the absolute limit, Nuala! What if she whips out a gun and demands the negatives?"

"Somehow I think she'll try an easier approach – money. I wonder how much she'll offer me for them," said Nuala, carefully placing the negatives between the pages of her passport, before returning it to the compartment on her body belt, where she kept her valuables.

"Would you sell them?" asked Judith in a surprised voice.

"Of course not, that would be assisting a crime," replied Nuala. "Honestly Judith, you have a very funny idea of me."

"Why don't you just throw them out?" said Aileen. "Or burn them with a match?"

"I don't think I'll destroy them yet, but when I do, it won't be either of those ways. I haven't a match, as it happens."

Josie gave a start and said, "I forgot to tell you, Miss Ryan says we are all to lie down and rest until the siesta is over. She's worried we'll get heatstroke or something."

Judith lay down on her bed. "It's not a bad idea," she said. "Do you realise we've really only two more days in Rome after today?"

"I wonder what we'll do tomorrow," said Aileen. "I know the day after will be the high point of the tour, visiting the Vatican and seeing the Pope."

"Not to mention St Peter's and all the other sights there, too," said Josie.

"I'm really looking forward to visiting the Sistine Chapel," said Judith. "Aren't we lucky they've finished the big cleaning job on it?"

Nuala looked over at Judith. "I see you haven't heard about the Pope and St Brigid's. When the glorious news reached him that we were coming to Rome, he immediately ordered a thorough scrub of the place and not only the Vatican either, remember what a good job they made of the Trevi Fountain?"

"I noticed quite a few of the other fountains had been cleaned up too," grinned Aileen. "And what about that big job they're doing on the roof of St Mary Major!"

The drowsy heat was beginning to have an effect on them. Judith yawned and said, "It's just occurred to me, Nuala, that while every other school just goes on tours, we have to get mixed up with industrial spies. That is, if your theory is correct."

"You surely can't have forgotten the curse an ancient Celtic hag placed on the Norman owner of St Brigid's, when it was still only a castle," said Nuala sleepily. "'Every hundred years, some maidens fair will have to right seven wrongs to clear the air', or words to that effect."

"Trust you to come up with a crazy answer and trust me to be the idiot to ask you," said Judith ruefully. "Wouldn't you agree, Aileen and Josie?"

Drowsy murmurs of assent came from the other beds. Judith lay back on the pillows. Soon she too fell asleep.

The loud banging of shutters from the shops on the street below them, signalling that the siesta was over, woke Aileen up. For a minute she lay there listening to the sound of cheerful voices and the noise of passing cars, as the area came to life again. "Come on, get up," she called to the others. "We're going shopping on the *Via Nazionale*, remember!"

Josie sat up, rubbing her eyes. "Imagine young 'uns like us falling asleep in the middle of the day. The shame of it," she said cheerfully, jumping out of bed.

"Is it true that Miss Ryan has arranged a meal for us in a *trattoria* this evening?" asked Nuala, as they left the room sometime later.

"Quite true," said Josie. "I had it from News of the World, E Murray herself."

The shopping trip was a great success especially with Miss Grimes, the fifth years and Gwendoline. It was on their way back that they came across the Basilica of Santa Prassede in one of the sidestreets quite near to their hotel.

"Santa Prassede was a daughter of the Roman senator Pudens, a friend of St Peter's," explained Miss Ryan. "There was a church here from the earliest times, but this one was built in the 9th century by Pope Pascal I."

"I've never heard of her," said Nuala. "Was she a martyr?"

"No, but her sister was. She collected the relics and blood of martyrs for veneration. There is a place marked in the floor of the church under which there is a well where, tradition tells us, she deposited the blood and relics of the martyrs."

To Miss Ryan's surprise, this Basilica proved almost to be the most popular with the girls so far. It wasn't so much the wonderful mosaics, carved crucifix and the stunning 9th century chapel of St Zeno, (so beautiful that it is known as the garden of paradise) that impressed them as much as the atmosphere in it. "It's hard to describe," said Josie. "It feels as if it's a parish church, where the locals have been coming for centuries to pray in."

"They still are," said Nuala. "When we were walking around looking at all the mosaics, I noticed quite a few people come in and light candles before that wooden crucifix in the old part of the church and kneel down to pray there."

"Isn't the crypt brilliant," said Fidelma. "It's so ancient. When I saw the four big stone coffins there and heard that they contained the relics of the saints, including Santa Prassede and her sister, all I could say was 'Wow'!"

"Don't forget the painting on one of the walls there," said Eithne. "The two saints on either side of Mary as Queen Mother look so sweet and pretty."

"I found the fragment of marble, that was brought to Rome at the end of the first crusade very interesting, as it's supposed to be a part of the pillar at which Christ was scourged," said Miss Ryan.

"Do you think that it really was?" asked Judith.

"I have no reason to doubt it. Cardinal Colonna, who brought it back, probably got it from Christians who had kept it as a revered relic all those centuries."

"This Basilica is full of art treasures," said Miss Grimes, as they all went out the door again. "We are very privileged indeed to have come across it."

Lisa, Sharon and the three other fifth years had been very impressed by the Basilica too. However, on their way back to the hotel the sight of *San Patricio's*, the Irish bar, had put everything out of their minds but the fact that they intended slipping out of the hotel again that night on a visit to it.

"It will have to be tonight," said Lisa. "It might be our only chance."

"Definitely," said Sharon. "We gave the old bag the slip easily enough last night. I'm looking forward to it. Gertie said the crack is brilliant there."

"What are you wearing?" asked Nessa.

"Either my black lace top or the black sleeveless mini-dress. We can have a try-on session when we get back," said Sharon.

"The great thing is that we won't even have to get a taxi, the bar is so near to our *via*," said Lisa.

"What time will we go?" asked Nessa.

"We'll wait till the others are back and the two teachers are in bed," said Sharon. "I suppose about ten-thirty or as they say here, twenty-two thirty."

This made her friends laugh so much that they never noticed Monica and Gwendoline walk swiftly past them and join the Murrays, who were going through the entrance door of the hotel.

Just before the third years were due to leave for their evening meal, Gwendoline complained to Monica that she couldn't find her hold-all with all her photographs and negatives in it anywhere.

"Did you try Nuala's room? Remember she was minding it for you," said Monica.

"Good idea," said Gwendoline. "I'll run down and see if she has it."

Nuala wasn't in her room when Gwendoline burst into it, but Judith good-naturedly searched for her, only to discover that all her own negatives were missing too.

"They've struck again," said Judith dramatically.

"Who has struck again?" asked Nuala coming into the room, while Aileen and Josie checked their cases and bags.

"Nuala, all our negatives have been taken," said Judith.

"Mine and Aileen's too," said Josie. "And Gwendoline's hold-all has gone with her negatives and photographs as well!"

"Wow, they have certainly struck," said Nuala, going over to where her belongings were. "I suppose mine have gone also."

"That's a bit much, I must say," she said a minute later, after a hasty search. "Everything's gone!"

"What are you talking about," asked a puzzled Gwendoline. "Who are 'they' and what are they taking our negatives for?"

"According to Nuala, a pair of industrial spies have been in our rooms, pinching our films," said Judith.

"Industrial spies! What are they?" asked poor Gwendoline, more puzzled than ever.

"It's a long story, Gwendoline," said Nuala. "You go back to your room and get ready. I'll explain everything on our way to this eating place."

Gwendoline looked as if she wanted to hear the story there and then, but Josie pushed her gently out of the room. "Don't worry, you'll hear everything later. Miss Ryan doesn't like being kept waiting."

As soon as she was gone, Josie asked Nuala, "Have you still got the real negatives?"

"I have, of course, safe and snug with my passport in my belt."

"Let's go," said Aileen, "we'll discuss it on the way to the *trattoria*."

12

Trattorias and Traps

It was with mixed feelings that the group set out for their evening meal. Some of them, notably the Murrays, would have much preferred to have gone to McDonald's, while others favoured the more *La Grotta Azzuria* type of place, large and lively. Miss Ryan warned them, as they walked the comparatively short distance to their destination, that *da Antonio* was a small unpretentious family trattoria mostly patronised by Italians. It had been highly recommended to her.

The first view of *da Antonio* with its half curtained door set between two modest windows didn't raise their spirits either. However, once inside they began to change their minds. There was something appealing in the sparkling cleanliness of the place, with shelves of quaintly-shaped wine bottles around the walls and rows of fat sausages and whole hams hanging from the ceiling. They were met by a middle-aged man, presumably Antonio, who greeted them with courteous *"Buona Sera"* and led them to their table at the back of the *trattoria*. Immediately, his son, wearing a long apron of dazzling whiteness, appeared beside them, pen in hand to take their orders.

Miss Ryan suggested for their first course *Melone e Prosciutto di Parma*. Antonio junior, a grave young man, instantly sprang up on a small step and took down one of the hams hanging from the ceiling. Then, producing a wicked looking knife, he swiftly carved about a dozen or so wafer-thin slices from it, before returning the ham to its hook.

"I like this place," said Aileen. "I think there's something specially nice about starchy white tablecloths and the china is very pretty too."

"I must tell Sr Gobnait," teased Nuala, "so she can have the refectory changed to suit your tastes. Would you like hams hanging from the ceiling and shelves of funny-shaped bottles of wine too?"

"White tablecloths and nice china will be sufficient, Nuala. Maybe you could include some of these salty cheese sticks on every table too," Aileen replied serenely, picking one of the sticks in question out of its glass jar and nibbling at it.

Melon e Prosciutto di Parma turned out to be some of the wafers of ham curled up beside a large wedge of very ripe melon. Miss Ryan hid a smile, as she listened to the unqualified approval this course received from the girls. She wondered what they would say if they knew that the ham, though specially cured, wasn't cooked at all.

After a lot of discussion, chicken was picked for the main course. "*Pollo alla Diavola*, sounds

111

fierce," said Nuala, "with I think *patate*, *funghi* and *fagiolini*."

"What the dickens are those?" asked Deirdre, who was sitting beside her.

"Grilled chicken, potatoes, mushrooms and French beans," laughed Nuala. "Turn the menu over – it's in English on the other side."

"I'll have the same," Deirdre said, "except for the French beans, I don't like them."

They had to point out the items on the menu to Antonio junior, as he didn't speak or understand English.

"Pollo, patate, funghi," he said gravely, then went off to the kitchen on winged feet.

"He's a real whizz kid, isn't he," said Josie. "Pity he can't smile, though."

Judith laughed. "His father is the same, they are very serious and dedicated, aren't they?" she said watching the older man bring out a large piece of raw steak to a customer, so that he could vet it before ordering.

"I wish I could speak Italian," said Nuala. "It's very frustrating not being able to communicate."

In due course Antonio junior arrived with plates of chicken which he served in his usual deft fashion. The vegetables came separately and soon they were all surrounded by little side dishes.

"Formaggio," Nuala heard at her side, and there he was again, this time placing a special jar of grated cheese on the table which he indicated she should sprinkle over her French beans.

"I have to tell you, Miss Ryan," Eithne was

saying at the other end of the table. "Much as I hate to admit it, the food is really good here, especially the chicken."

The teacher was pleased. "I'm very glad to hear that," she said smiling. "It would have been a shame to have travelled all the way to Rome and then only eat at McDonald's.

"I'm not saying that I would prefer it. I miss the chips, for instance. These slices of potato in oil aren't bad, but they're no substitute," said Eithne hastily.

"Wait till you to see the *Gelato di Fragole*, strawberry ice cream, you'll want to come again," said Miss Ryan, laughing at the expression on Eithne's face which she had correctly interpreted.

The *Gelato di Fragole* was all the teacher had promised. Even Josie, previously disillusioned by Italian ice cream, agreed that it was brilliant. The meal had taken longer than expected, so they didn't linger over their cappuccino. Then with smiles and thanks they paid the bill and left the *trattoria*.

"*Arrivederci e grazie,*" called the Antonios punctiliously before returning quickly to their work.

"I think I'd like a walk," said Miss Ryan. "We'll go over towards *Via Merulana* and up towards *Santa Maria Maggiore*, before we go back to thehotel. All right, girls?"

Nobody had any objections to a walk so they set off, the teacher leading the way with Monica and Deirdre and the rest falling in behind them.

The traffic augmented by motor-bikes and mopeds seemed even noisier than usual, but the streets were free from pedestrians; the only person they passed was a man exercising a large Alsatian.

"Everyone must be still eating their supper," said Josie. "Or else watching TV."

"It's a nice change having the pavements to ourselves," said Aileen.

They passed quickly from one street, turning into another one, which hadn't as many shops or offices as elsewhere. As they walked along it, they could see high walls with great doors set in them every now and again.

"I wonder what's behind those doors," said Judith. "They must be twelve feet high at least."

"Warehouses or art galleries," suggested Nuala idly, her mind on the stolen negatives. It was a horrible thought that these crooks could get into their rooms whenever they wished to. Nuala, feeling quite guilty about this, was half-deciding to tell Miss Ryan the whole story, when she heard Judith say, "There's one of these doors opening up just ahead of us, let's hurry and see what's behind them."

Evidently Aileen and Josie shared Judith's curiosity, for when Nuala and Judith, who had been walking faster than everyone, arrived at the open door, the other two were close behind them. Nuala and Judith stepped off the pavement, peering around the massive metal door, where they were surprised to see a large courtyard, with a tall house to one side of it and an ornamental fountain in the middle of it.

114

"Wow!" said Josie from behind. "I never would have expected that."

"Quick, get back," said Judith. "There's a car coming."

They pulled back out of sight, not anxious to be caught peeping into someone's private garden. A large black car drove slowly out on to the street and turned in the opposite direction, gathered speed and was soon out of sight. It appeared to be driven by a man, with two women in the back seat. Even though the girls were so close to the car, they couldn't see what the occupants looked like in the failing light. The big doors slowly closed over and they were free to go on.

"Did you see that, Miss Ryan?" enthused Aileen.

"There was a house and courtyard with a fountain behind those doors. Would you have guessed that?"

"No," said the teacher. "Rome is certainly full of surprises. They seem to live among the shops and offices here, very sensible of them too."

It didn't take much longer to reach the wide street which Miss Ryan had mentioned, *Via Merulana*. "It was built by Pope Sixtus to connect the two Basilicas – Santa Mary Major on our left and St John Lateran far away down on the right. We'll have to visit St John Lateran tomorrow, our time in Rome is nearly up, alas."

"This week has gone like the wind," said Eithne. "That's always the way when you're enjoying yourself."

"Wouldn't it be great if you could hold the good moments for ages and rush through the bad times?" said Nuala.

"You mean like that time when Mork visited *Happy Days* and froze time," said Josie. "The only trouble is you'd never want to give up the good times."

They walked along the *Via Merulana* until the Basilica of Santa Mary Major loomed up before them, its floodlit outlines making it appear curiously ghostlike and ephemeral in the dark night. Turning, they went back to the traffic lights which they passed on their way down to the street on which their hotel was situated.

They met Miss Grimes in the foyer in the hotel, where she detained them with eager questions about their visit to *da Antonio*. As they stood around waiting until she was finished, the desk clerk came over and handed Judith a rather battered looking hold-all. "One of the cleaners left this here for you."

"For me!" she said in surprise, then she noticed Gwendoline's name on it. "It's not mine, but I know who owns it, I'll give it to her."

Miss Grimes moved away at last. Judith rushed over to Gwendoline, gave her the hold-all, hissing at her not to screech until the teachers were out of earshot. A short time later Judith and Nuala went down to Gwendoline's room, where they found the Murrays, Monica and Deirdre chattering excitedly, while Gwendoline, looking dazed, tried ineffectually to sort out the jumbled heaps of negatives which lay on her bed.

116

"I don't know what to do," she said weakly. "As far as I can see they just bundled everybody's negatives back into my bag."

"Don't bother," said Nuala, appalled at the mess on the bed. "Wait until we get home, you'll have more time to sort it all out then."

Gwendoline, looking relieved, shovelled it all back into her hold-all, quickly zipping it up.

"It looks as if you're right, Nuala," said Judith. "They really want those negatives."

"Of course they do," said Nuala. "There are simply thousands of pounds or dollars or more likely millions of lira at stake.

"Come on, Nuala, we'd better go back to our own room, it's nearly ten p.m. Aileen and Josie will think that we are lost."

Eithne looked at her watch, then jumped up and pushed them towards the door. "Go at once," she said. "Miss Grimes will be here soon."

"Keep your hair on," said Nuala. "We're going, we know when we're not wanted."

As soon as the two friends had left the room, Eithne picked up a guidebook, quickly flicking through it until she reached the language section. "Here it is, *ferma* means stop, *aspelta* means wait and *adesso* means now. I hope I remember those three."

"Now," said Fidelma, picking up two torches, one of which she gave to her twin, "it's getting very near the time, do you all know what to do?"

"We all go down to the second floor and hide out of sight of the stairs," said Monica.

"I hold the lift for the quick getaway," said Gwendoline.

"When Monica gives the signal, I turn off the lights," said Fidelma.

"Then I do my bit with the torch," said Eithne.

"What happens if the lift is in use?" asked Gwendoline.

"Use your head, we go down in it and hold it. Thank goodness this is a small hotel and has only one lift," replied Eithne.

"Make it snappy, Eithne," said her twin. "Whatever happens, you lot, don't give the game away that it was us."

Twenty-five minutes later, the five of them, dressed in black T-shirts and leggings, left the room, their runners making no sound on the carpeted floors of the ancient building, which had been acquired as an overflow hotel only a year or two previously. The new owners had modernised as much as possible, but nothing could change the high-ceilinged narrow little passages which linked the rooms on every floor, or the steep windowless staircase which twisted its way through the hotel.

13

Tricks and Threats

Eithne and her room-mates had hardly got into the lift, when the door of the fifth year bedroom opened slowly. Sharon peeped out. "All clear," she whispered. "We'll go by the stairs, it will be safer, the *Cleaner* always uses the lift."

"She must be in her room by now," said Lisa, appearing beside her. "But using the stairs is a good idea all the same."

When the last girl was out in the corridor, Sharon carefully locked the bedroom door, placing the key in her money belt. "I don't want to hand it into the desk," she said in a low voice. "We'll have to slip out of the hotel without anyone seeing us."

The hotel was very quiet and the fifth years, creeping silently down the rather inadequately-lit staircase, didn't see or hear anyone. Which wasn't any surprise to them, as naturally no one used the stairs when there was a lift to go by. Reaching the second floor they turned into a narrow passage with a large mirror taking up most of the wall at the end of it. The light suddenly dimmed, effectively slowing down their progress.

"Who are those weirdos?" whispered Nessa, pointing to where she could see wild-looking faces staring at them.

"Don't be silly. It's only us in that mirror," said Sharon crossly.

Someone seemed to move out from the mirror, then a strong beam of light shone in their eyes. Dazzled, they retreated a little.

"Ferma, Aspelta Adesso!" called a deep harsh voice. *"Ferma pronto!"* it ordered. "Where do you think you are going, evil ones? I shall report you to the proper authorities."

As they huddled together quite terrified, wondering who the mad person was, the dazzling light was withdrawn. The person merged back into the mirror and disappeared.

Sometime earlier Miss Grimes, who had just finished an unexpected but welcome phone call, came cheerfully out of the booth in the foyer, making straight for the lift. Having been unsuccessful in summoning it after five minutes with her finger on the button, she felt her good humour begin to dissipate. After further fruitless efforts she looked around for the night clerk but he seemed to have vanished. In desperation, she started to mount the stairs feeling extremely bad-tempered.

As she reached the top of the first flight of stairs and turned into the passageway, she did not at first recognise the very frightened girls standing there, looking as if they were carved from stone. In fact she was about to pass them, when suddenly she realised who they were.

"Lisa, Sharon and you, Nellie," she called sharply. At that they came to life, running noisily back to the stairs in an effort to get away. Inspiration came to the teacher and she ran downstairs again. This time the lift was waiting for her, she stepped in and was soon whisked up to the top floor.

As she stepped out of the lift, the five breathless red-faced fifth years appeared from the stairs and ran right into her path. "Ha!" she said truimphantly. "Come to my room at once and explain yourselves. When I checked you at twenty-two hours you were all in bed. You said you were very tired and about to go to sleep." She turned and went into her room, the fifth years following in her wake. The combination of the apparition in the passage and that mad rush up those awful stairs had knocked all the stuffing out of them.

Eithne, peeping out the door of her room, retreated in amazement at the sight of the five girls she had last seen cowering in a narrow passage on the second floor. They were now meekly walking behind Miss Grimes as she went into her room.

Closing and locking the door carefully, she turned to her room-mates, her eyes popping. "Wow," she said. "You'll never believe this. They've been caught and by the *Cleaner* herself, how did that happen, I wonder?"

"We'll never find that out," said Fidelma. "But at least we know that they've been nobbled, the great twits."

"I hope they don't find out about our part in it," said Monica nervously. "They'd never forgive us."

"We'd better be careful not to say anything to anyone about our little game," said Eithne.

"Not even to Nuala, Aileen or Judith?" asked Monica in amazement.

"You know I'd love to tell them, they would enjoy the joke, but we must be careful," said Eithne. "Better wait for a day or two, all the same."

In the teachers' room across the passage Miss Grimes was grilling the fifth years about their conduct in sneaking down the stairs after room check. Sharon, who had recovered by now, explained earnestly. "It was all my fault. I just couldn't sleep, it was so hot, so I thought I would go down and watch TV in the lounge. I was hoping there would be a wildlife programme on as it wouldn't matter then that I didn't know the language."

"I couldn't let her go on her own," Lisa said quickly. "It wouldn't have been right."

Miss Grimes looked at their faces, twisted into expressions of devoted concern. She wasn't quite sure what to believe. "You'd better go back to bed," she said grimly. "But this time stay there."

"Yes, Miss Grimes," they said, meekly filing out of the room. Miss Ryan came in then.

"What was their story?" she asked with keen interest.

The older teacher told her, adding, "I don't

believe a word of it but there's nothing I can really do, especially as they were still on the premises."

Back in their own room the disappointed fifth years started reluctantly to get ready for bed."Somebody shopped us," said Lisa. "If I knew who did it, I'd string them up."

Sharon, who was brushing her hair, stopped and looked with narrowed eyes at Lisa. "I have been thinking since we came in here," she said, "and I know now who did it. Nuala O'Donnell! She has always hated me."

"How do you know that it was Nuala?" asked Lisa."She couldn't have known what we were going to do."

"Who else in that stupid crowd of third years would have the neck to play that trick on us?" said Sharon angrily. "The question is, what are we going to do about it?"

"Tell Miss Grimes that we are worried about Nuala and Judith's behaviour. You know, chatting up boys everywhere they go," said Lisa.

"No, she'd never believe us. We'll have to think of something more subtle than that," said Sharon.

"What about a letter supposed to be from some guys to Nuala, going by accident to the *Cleaner*?" suggested Lisa.

"I like the idea of a letter," said Sharon.

"I know, why don't we send a threatening letter to Nuala warning her that we know that she split on us and that we are planning a fearful revenge. That will give her a good fright," said Nessa.

123

Sharon liked this idea so, fishing out a piece of paper and a pen, she sat down to sketch out a rough draft. After several attempts and a lot of wasted paper, she produced a letter which satisfied the five of them.

"You don't think we should sign it?" said Colette.

"No, that would be stupid and give us away if she showed it to anyone," said Sharon impatiently. "This way she'll know and be worried but can't prove a thing either."

"How are you going to get it to her?" asked Nessa. "We can't very well go up and hand it to her."

"She's right. Sharon, have you any ideas?" said Lisa.

"I'll just leave it on the reception desk," said Sharon. "They'll give it to her. I'll put the room number on it too so that it won't go wrong."

"As well as St Brigid's, of course," said Nessa, then remembering how terrified she had been in the passage, she added crossly. "I hope it really upsets her."

Lisa laughed. "Of course it will, 'specially when she sees us staring at her thoughtfully every time we meet."

"We never meet them," protested Colette. "They're always finished breakfast and away before we even have ours."

"You're forgetting the day after tomorrow. The whole crowd of us are going together to the Vatican," said Sharon, impatiently. She didn't like

Colette questioning her.

"I still think roughing up their room or making trouble for her with the teachers could be good fun," said Lisa, who had been looking forward to a bit of crack in the Irish bar.

"I don't agree," said Sharon, "with our luck, we'd probably get caught and get into worse trouble. This is the best way."

Colette had been right about one thing: on the following morning when they arrived down for breakfast, they discovered that Miss Ryan and the third years had left some time earlier to visit the Basilica of St John Lateran, which was quite near to the hotel. Sharon didn't let it worry her. When she had gone to the reception desk, on her way to breakfast, the clerk was sorting the post, so she just slipped it among the letters there when his back was turned.

About an hour later Miss Ryan was in the Basilica of St John Lateran showing the famous painting by Giotto, (on one of the inside walls), to her troop. "It was painted in the year thirteen hundred," said the teacher, "to commemorate the first Holy Year. See, there's Pope Boniface looking at St Peter's."

"Excuse me, Miss Ryan," came an anguished whisper from Gwendoline. "My camera, I left it behind in the hotel."

"Oh no, Gwendoline, we'll have to go back. Fortunately we've been all over the Basilica already," said the teacher who was worried that Gwendoline's valuable camera might be stolen.

It didn't take them long to walk back to the hotel. Once there, Gwendoline rushed inside, followed more slowly by Miss Ryan.

"Let's go and get some ice cream, while we're waiting," suggested Aileen.

"Good idea," said Josie. "We can go to the shop at the corner."

When they came back happily licking, they met a beaming Gwendoline, camera in hand, walking out of the hotel with Miss Ryan who was putting a letter away into her bag. Handing another letter to Nuala, she said, "Here you are Nuala, this is for you. I found it among my post."

"Thank you, Miss Ryan," said Nuala, wondering who could have written to her. She tore the envelope open and found a single sheet of paper in it:

You think you're smart, don't you? Well, we're on to you. Beware. We'll be everywhere watching you at all times. When we're ready, we'll strike you hard

Nudging Judith's arm, she said in a low voice, "Read this and pass it on to Aileen and Josie, but don't say anything. I don't want the others to know."

Judith, looking startled, took the piece of paper and read it, then passed it to Aileen with Nuala's warning. "What do you think of that?" Nuala asked Judith as they walked down the street behind Miss Ryan.

"You must be right about them. They are really

126

desperate to get those negatives, aren't they?" Judith replied.

Aileen and Josie hung back until they were beside Nuala and Judith. "Wow, they really mean business. What are you going to do?" asked Josie.

"I don't know," said Nuala frankly. "I'll have to think about it, but keep your eyes peeled for that pair."

"We will," they all said fervently. None of them thought of looking up at the apartments above the shops they were passing, or they would have seen a woman dressed in black, who was sitting at an open window glaring down at them as they passed along.

14

The Pantheon, Past and Present

"Pantheon, a greek word meaning 'all the gods' was originally built as a temple to the gods between 27 – 25 BC," Miss Ryan read out to the third years sitting around her, lazily watching the famous fountains in the *Piazza Navona* and enjoying the sun. "The present temple was rebuilt by the Emperor Hadrian about 120 AD. Its perfect state of preservation is due to the fact that Pope Boniface IV consecrated it as a church in 608 AD to St Mary and all the Martyrs."

"Is it true that the painter Raphael is buried there?" asked Judith. "I'd like to see his grave."

"That's right, Judith, quite a few artists are buried there, but Raphael is the most famous. Anyway, to continue, the great sense of harmony of the interior is due to its perfect proportions, the diameter is the same as the height, 140 ft."

Gwendoline jumped up. "Miss Ryan, I just have to take a photo of you and the girls with that fountain behind you. It would be a perfect one to keep in memory of our tour," she said, pointing to the fountain of the rivers, before enthusiastically positioning her camera.

Miss Ryan laughed, putting away the guide book. "Go ahead, Gwendoline, and take it," she said. "I suppose you are all bored hearing about historic buildings, but I wanted to give you some idea of the Pantheon's history before we visit it." Most of the girls hastened to reassure her, but the rest were quite glad of the interruption, especially as some of them wanted to take photographs as well. They realised that it would be their last chance. As soon as the photographic session was finished, Miss Ryan got up and they started on their way again.

"First of all, we'll visit the Pantheon," she said as they walked slowly across the piazza. "It's really our last day to see places around here. Tomorrow, as you know, we will be going to the Vatican. I think each of you should pick a place to visit today."

"The Spanish Steps for me," said Monica.

"And me too," said Deirdre.

"McDonald's, definitely, for our meal," said the Murrays.

To the teacher's surprise, Nuala, Judith and Aileen wanted to go shopping as well as Gwendoline. "Well, Josie, have you any wishes?" asked Miss Ryan. "You're the last."

"I'd like a surprise," said Josie. "Something different and unexpected."

"That's a tall order," laughed the teacher. "If we've time, there is somewhere I would like to see that might fulfil your request, Josie, but more about that later."

It may have been that letter preying on her mind, but as they left the *piazza* and went down a small *via* on their way to the Pantheon Nuala felt, rather that saw, a somewhat familiar face staring at them from a shop window. She didn't mention it to anyone, even though it worried her.

It didn't take long to reach the Pantheon. Looking at the rows of classical columns forming the entrance porch there Aileen said, "There's something very familiar about this place."

"I'm not surprised," said Nuala. "A lot of courthouses in Ireland have fronts like that, the Four Courts in Dublin, for instance."

"Dundalk courthouse has one too," said Deirdre.

As they were passing into the circular hall which is the body of the church, Josie thought she heard someone call her name. Turning, she saw with amazement her cousin Connor waving to her from one of the columns in the porch. Pushing her way through the people pouring in and out of the ancient building, she eventually reached him and greeted him affectionately. He could only talk to her for a minute as his group were already on their way to the nearby Church of *St Maria Sopra Minerva* where St Catherine of Sienna is buried.

"Who was that?" asked Aileen, who had waited for her.

"What a lucky break," said Josie, rather breathlessly. "That was my cousin, he's on his school tour too; St Paul's, Navan. They have seen at least half a dozen places already today as they've only two days in Rome."

"Wow, where are they going then?" asked Aileen.

"Florence, Assisi, Naples and this will make you really jealous, two days in Capri," replied Josie.

"Lucky things, I wouldn't like the rest of their tour though," said Aileen. "It would just be rush rush all the time and far too much travelling in the coach for me."

"I like our tour better as well," said Josie. "But wasn't it brilliant meeting him here, a chance in a million, you could call it."

They found Nuala and Judith standing in front of Raphael's tomb. "He was only 37 years old when he died," said Judith in a reverent hushed voice. "But what brilliant art treasures he left behind him."

"What do you think of this place then?" asked Nuala hastily, catching a certain look on Aileen's face. "Miss Ryan says it has changed little since ancient times, I suppose they must have got rid of all the old pagan statues though, when it was turned into a church."

"I suppose so," said Josie. "It has a very calm churchy feeling about it all the same, look at the altar and the tombs."

"Well it's been a church for, let me see," said Nuala, "about 1300 years, it should feel like one."

"Why did you three say you wanted to go shopping?" asked Josie. "I thought you'd got all your presents already."

"Judith suggested that we should buy something for Miss Ryan," said Nuala. "I'm sure everyone will go in on it, that way we can buy something really decent."

"Great idea," agreed Josie. "She's been super to us all week. I've really enjoyed Rome."

"That's what I feel too," said Judith, pleased that the others had agreed with her.

"The roof is leaking," said Aileen, pointing to a pool of water on the floor a little distance from them.

"She's right," said Nuala, watching a big drop of water fall from the dome to the floor. "Well, this place is very old. Can you imagine how we'd function if we were going since 27 BC?"

"Yes, indeed," laughed Josie. "By the way, now that we are alone, if surrounded by dozens, what about that letter you got this morning, Nuala?"

"You mean *Beware we are watching you*?" said Aileen. "It sounds as if they are trying to frighten you."

"Well, I didn't pay much attention to it at first," said Nuala. "Then when we were leaving the *piazza Navona*, I thought I saw someone familiar peering out of a shop at me. It gave me quite a fright."

"Was it the man with the sad eyes?" asked Josie.

"I'm not sure but I think it was," said Nuala slowly.

Deirdre came over to them. "Miss Ryan says that we should go now. She feels Eithne and Fidelma are getting hungry."

Aileen laughed. "You'd think that they were a pair of mastiffs or something," she said.

"The Murray hounds must be fed," joked Nuala "or they will turn nasty. I'm hungry myself. Let's go, gang."

"I'll talk to the twins about the present for Miss Ryan as we go along," said Judith. "What about the other three?"

"That's easy enough," said Aileen. "I'll tackle Deirdre, Nuala, you speak to Gwendoline."

"I'll take care of Monica," said Josie.

They set off quite soon after that with the intention of going straight to McDonald's for something to eat, but in the end it didn't work out that way at all.

They walked along the busy crowded streets catching tantalising glimpses of the huge variety of goods displayed in the passing shops. Everyone wanted to stop for a closer look, especially Gwendoline, who still had presents to get for some of her family back home. Miss Ryan was agreeable, so they went into the next big store. Here Gwendoline, in obedience to a prearranged plan hastily worked out earlier as they left the Pantheon, asked the teacher and Monica to come and help her pick a gift for her grandmother.

The remainder of the girls immediately went around looking for something for Miss Ryan. Fortunately, Judith and Nuala stumbled on a jewellery counter which had a good selection and which was within the limitations of their funds. After a lot of discussion and even argument, a pair of earrings was found that they all felt was suitable enough to show the teacher their appreciation of her.

Paying and packaging didn't take too long and Nuala stowed the precious parcel away in her bag. Then, feeling very pleased with themselves, the seven of them went in search of the other three.

As soon as they appeared, Gwendoline, who had been trying to make up her mind between several items, declared that she didn't think any of them were suitable. "I'll leave it until we go to the Vatican tomorrow," she informed her two advisors. "Granny might prefer something religious and there's bound to be lots of things there."

"Good idea," said Monica, looking at the winks and nods Deirdre was giving her and correctly guessing that their mission was accomplished. "I bet she would like a pair of rosary beads, something like that anyway."

The heat hit them as they left the shop, Aileen and Nuala leading the way at a smart pace. Judith, who had been delayed by Monica and Gwendoline asking about the present for Miss Ryan, suddenly started weaving her way determinedly through the crowd. She caught up with Nuala, grabbing her arm. "Don't bother looking now because you couldn't see her anyway," she hissed, "but she's around watching us!"

Nuala looked at Judith. "Are you feeling all right?" she asked. "Who is this person who is watching us?"

"The woman in the garden of course, the one

134

who pinched our negatives," said Judith impatiently. "She was outside the shop when we left it, pretending to be window shopping."

Nuala stopped in her tracks, nearly causing an accident. "Oh no, I don't believe you," she said. "I feel hunted, are you sure?"

Judith nodded. "Yes, I'm sure," she said.

"How can she follow us around, doesn't she have a job to go to?" said Aileen.

"It's siesta time, remember," said Judith. "A lot of places close then, but how did she know we were here?"

"I just don't care any more," said Nuala. "I'm dying for a cold drink, let's hurry up and get to McD's, we can talk about it there."

Everybody must have felt the same as Nuala that day, for on arrival at the restaurant they found long queues of people stretching from the counters almost to the exit. They said nothing, just joined the queue.

Despite the noise and confusion, it didn't take very long to get served as there were dozens dishing out the food. Soon, with their trays laden with the day's special, they were beating a way down the stairs where they were told there were free tables. Nuala dumped her tray on one table in a little alcove conveniently empty and Aileen on another so as to secure it for the others who were still queueing for food.

"Thank goodness, that saved my life," said Nuala, putting down a half-empty glass. "These chips look brilliant."

Josie arrived with her tray, soon followed by all the others with Miss Ryan arriving last. There was silence for some time, as they wolfed down the eagerly-awaited food.

"Was that good!" said Eithne. "I was so hungry I could have eaten somebody's leg."

"Talk about going from the sublime to the ridiculous," said Miss Ryan. "One minute we were enjoying the classical beauty of the Pantheon and the next, Nuala and Aileen rushed us in here to fill up with chips and burgers or whatever."

"That's a Roman holiday for you," said Fidelma. "Food for the mind and soul alternating with food for the tum."

When they were all finished and leaving the restaurant Josie said, "Now, Miss Ryan, the others have all got their wish for today, what about mine. Something unexpected, a surprise!"

15

Felix and Frolics

"Oh, Josie," said Miss Ryan. "It isn't that I had forgotten about you, but I'm not sure that my idea would have been such a nice surprise for you really."

"I'm sure it would," said Josie. "Tell me anyway what it is."

Before the teacher could reply she felt a hand on her arm and a voice said, "What a coincidence. It is you, Vanessa, isn't it?"

Startled, she spun around. "Why, Felix," she said to the tall young man smiling at her. "What brings you here?"

He laughed. "Sightseeing, what else. I'll be going back home on Monday, so I thought I would get a few places done today."

"So your work is finished then?" she said. "Are you satisfied with it?"

"Yes, thank goodness. Everything is settled nicely with just a few papers to be signed. How are you getting on?" he asked, nodding towards the girls who had retired a few yards away from them.

"Fine," she said, then dropping her voice, she

asked, "Have you any ideas for a surprise, not sightseeing? I can't think of a thing."

He thought for a moment. "It's such a hot day, what about a swim?" he suggested. "You can go by underground to *Lido di Ostia*. I don't know anything about it, except that it is a beach."

"Brilliant," she said. "They'd love that. Come over here, girls," she called. When they had arrived beside her, she asked, "How many of you have swim suits with you?" It appeared everyone had, but of course they were back in their rooms at the hotel.

"Don't worry," said Felix. "We'll take a couple of taxis to the hotel and pick them up. It won't take long."

"Good idea, Felix, then we can go to the *Termini* for the *metro*, it's not too far from the hotel," said the teacher.

"Where are we going?" asked Nuala, Josie and Deirdre simultaneously.

Miss Ryan laughed. "Didn't I tell you? We're going for a swim in the Mediterranean sea!"

"What a brilliant surprise!" said Josie. "I couldn't think of a nicer one."

There was no shortage of taxis in the *Piazza di Spagne* and in a short time they were travelling back to their hotel. Felix elected to go with them for, as he explained, they would need him to look after their belongings on the beach while they went in for a swim. No one minded him coming, quite the reverse.

As soon as they reached the hotel everyone hurried in to get their gear, while Felix and Miss

Ryan paid the taxi man. When she was collecting her key from the desk clerk, Nuala was surprised to find a note with it. Opening it as they were going up in the lift she read:

Signora Fioretti rang. She wishes to speak with you. She will contact you again.

"This is from Miss Keane," she said to Aileen and Josie who were with her. "I wonder why she asked for me and not one of the teachers."

"Probably because she doesn't know them," said Aileen. "They only came to St Brigid's after she left."

"You know how batty she was too," said Josie. "Maybe she will invite us to visit the mansion or whatever they call it here. Wasn't her husband supposed to be loaded?"

"According to Gwendoline, the Fioretti are one of the richest families in Italy," said Aileen.

"I'm dying to see does she still wear the fur boots," said Nuala as they got out of the lift and went towards their room. "I think I'll tell them at the desk to tell her if she rings again that we'll be in the Vatican all day tomorrow but we'll be free the following morning."

The *metro* was crowded but the journey didn't take too long. On arrival the excited party picked their way between rows and rows of sun worshippers until they found a suitable spot on the gritty sand for themselves.

"It's a bit stony, isn't it?" said Aileen, rapidly undressing. "Not to mention all those millions of shells!"

"I hope the sea isn't lukewarm," said Josie. "I'm looking forward to a refreshing swim."

"Don't forget your sunblock," warned Gwendoline. "Or we'll be burnt dreadfully."

Soon they were all ready to go in. "Leave all your money belts and valuables with me," said Vanessa Ryan lazily from the reclining chair, one of two which Felix had hired on arrival for them.

"Leave your clothes fairly near too," said Felix. "A friend of mine, an American priest, went for a swim on a beach some distance from Rome. When he had his swim he thought he'd like an ice cream so he went across the beach and got one and when he returned to where he had left his clothes, he was horrified to find everything was gone, not even a vest left. He then had to go out and try and hitch a lift, in his bathing suit, mind you. After several hours he managed to persuade a lorry driver to take him to Rome where he was staying in one of the houses of his order. He was scarred by the experience, poor fellow!"

"What a ghastly story," said Vanessa. "Go on girls, I'll protect your clothes."

There was silence after the third years had gone happily into the sea. Vanessa adjusted her recliner, so that she could keep an eye on them all the time. Much as she liked having Felix's company, she had no intention of neglecting her duty.

"What sights did you see this morning?" she asked him.

"Oh the usual, Pantheon, Colosseum, Forum, Trevi Fountain," he said. "What about you?"

"We started with St John Lateran and then the Pantheon. We're going to the Vatican tomorrow," she said. "It's really our last day as we return on the three p.m. plane to Ireland on the day after tomorrow. It's been a full week, but I've really enjoyed this trip to Rome."

"I'm glad," he said simply. "They seem nice kids too."

"They're a great crowd. I'm lucky. Dottie Grimes, the other teacher, has a handful in her lot. Did you ever get to see the rooms of St Ignatius Loyola? Do you remember, you were talking about them."

"I did. They are well worth a visit. Only recently restored to their original style of over four hundred years ago, they are very small and simple with things like his own desk where he wrote letters to people all over the world, seven thousand in all I believe, apart from documents and spiritual writings."

"Wow," she said impressed. "I bet his writing was tiny too, they all seemed to write as if spiders had fallen in ink and run across the pages in those days. Paper was precious, of course."

"You're right," he said. "They were a bit like that, that is, the ones they had on show. It was extraordinary to look out through the window, the shutters are original and to see the same little garden that Ignatius saw and of course the very place on the floor where he died."

141

"I'm sorry we missed that. Was there anything else belonging to him there?"

"There were other things, but the things that impressed me most were his cloak and his shoes. When I was there they had it hanging on a peg with his shoes on the floor underneath. It gave a marvellous impression as if he had just come in, hung it up and gone into the other room to write or pray."

"I gave them all a chance to pick where they wanted to go today. Josie wanted a surprise. I had half-thought of the Ignatian rooms, but then they had seen so much this week, I decided not to. You saved my life, Felix, this visit to the beach was an inspiration."

"Don't give it a thought. I was very glad to meet you, Vanessa. I'm enjoying myself," he said. Changing the subject he asked, "Do you notice the way whole families walk along the beach together, father, mother, children and even granny. They still seem to have a great feeling for the family in Italy."

"Yes, I noticed that in the *trattoria* too," she replied, looking to where she could see a swarthy-faced individual who was waving his hands in the air as he talked earnestly to Judith and Nuala.

As she watched, the other girls came out of the sea and then they all ran up laughing and talking.

"The sea was cold," said Gwendoline, taking her towel and draping it around her shoulders. "I thought it would have been warm here."

"It takes you by surprise all right," said Aileen.

"I suppose it's the contrast between it and the hot sun."

"It was brilliantly refreshing," said Josie. She spread her towel on the sand and lay down on it. "Do you think I could get a quick tan this way?"

"What was that man saying to you, Nuala?" asked Vanessa Ryan.

"The one who looked like Anthony Quinn, the film star, dark and craggy-faced?" said Nuala laughing. "He saw Judith rubbing suntan lotion on her arms and came pushing in with some advice."

"'Throw that rubbish way,' he said. 'Do as we do, splasha da sea all over you, let it dry and then splasha da sea again and again'," said Judith, grinning. "He waved his hands in demonstration each time too."

"Your poor skin," said Gwendoline, shuddering. "All that sea and sun would make it like leather."

"It's all right for the Italians, only us fair celtic beauties would burn horribly," said Nuala, "but he meant well."

"I see some stalls over there selling food," said Eithne. "Fidelma and I would like to go over and see if there is anything nice in them."

Felix got up. "I would like a drink, can I get anything for you Vanessa?" he asked.

"A cold drink would be lovely," she said. "I'm too lazy to get up or even move, I'm so comfortable here."

In the end the Murrays, Monica, Deirdre and

Aileen set off with Felix to get the refreshments, not only for themselves but for the others who stayed behind. When they were gone the rest anointed themselves with sunblock and chatted in low voices, except for the teacher, who appeared to be asleep.

"What do you think of you know who?" asked Judith.

"I think he's OK. Would you say there's anything between them?" said Josie.

"It's hard to know," said Nuala. "But I'm glad he turned up, especially after we had brought her present and were free to come here."

"Yes, the timing was good," said Judith. "We're going to have an awful job getting all this sand out of our clothes, the hotel won't like it if we drop it all over the stairs and rooms."

"We must buy a card tomorrow to go with the present," said Nuala. "And I must send dozens of cards to Ireland tomorrow too. Everyone will expect one."

"It's a crazy time to send them, the day before you leave," said Josie.

"No matter when you send them, they don't arrive for ages afterwards," said the experienced Gwendoline, "so it really doesn't matter."

"Here they come," said Nuala, "and they seem to have got plenty. Thank goodness. It must be the sea air but I feel parched!"

It wasn't long before the foraging party were back with cans of drink, melons, ice creams, peanuts and crisps, all of which were appreciated, especially the melons.

144

Aileen handed Nuala a large piece of melon and sat down on the sand beside her. "You won't believe this," she said. "But on our way back with the grub, we passed some of the boys who were sunbathing. They looked perfectly tanned to me, then someone noticed that they were using cones of foil of some sort to direct the sunrays to parts it mightn't reach on its own."

"You're not serious," said Nuala. "This melon is delicious . . . but whereabouts were they directing the sun?"

"Under their arms, according to Monica, and behind their knees!" said Aileen.

"Yuk," said Josie. "What a funny thing to do. Imagine making special cones to do it with!"

"They obviously take their suntanning very seriously," said Nuala. "I've never heard of that method before."

About an hour later, Miss Ryan decided that it was time to go. Accordingly they left *Lido di Ostia* shaking the sand from themselves as well as they could.

When they reached the Metro, they had to say goodbye to Felix as he was going in another direction. "Goodbye and thanks a million for everything," Vanessa said warmly to him. "You made the day for all of us, but especially Josie."

He clasped her hands in his. "It made my day too. I'll be in touch next week. All right?"

She smiled. "All right. I'll be looking forward to that."

Then he went away to a chorus of 'thank you' Felix' from the girls, interested bystanders.

A very crabbed Miss Grimes met them at the hotel entrance. "Where have you been?" she said, looking at their dishevelled appearance and rolled-up wet towels.

"The beach and swimming in the sea – I've never heard of such behaviour on a tour to Rome before!"

16

The Pigeons of St Peter's

"It doesn't look real, does it?" said Nuala on the following morning as they stood in the middle of St Peter's *Piazza* and looked at the famous Basilica in front of them.

"I've seen it so often on TV. I can't believe I'm here. I must be dreaming."

"Give her a good pinch, Aileen, and that will wake her up!" said Josie. "Look at the people going in and out the main door of the Basilica. They look the size of ants!"

"Come on, girls, let's join the ants," said Miss Ryan from behind them. "I want to see some of St Peter's before we go to our audience with the Pope."

The rest of the St Brigid's party, who had travelled with them to the Vatican, had now all alighted from the coach and were going off in small groups. At Miss Ryan's words, the third years fell in beside her, walking up the long entrance steps to the main door of the Basilica. "That's where the pope lives," the teacher said, pointing to the building on their right just behind Bernini's famous columns.

"Would you say he's looking out of his window at us as we pass?" asked Josie.

"I bet he is, saying to himself, 'Brilliant, St Brigid's have arrived at last!'" joked Nuala.

"I'm glad to hear it," said Josie, unabashed.

Once inside the Basilica, Miss Ryan led them to the right where Michelangelo's famous statue of the dead Christ in his Mother's arms, called the *Pieta*, is to be found. It was enclosed in a bullet-proof glass case because some deranged person attacked it with a hammer in the seventies. "Michangelo was only twenty-four years old when he carved it out of a single block of marble" explained Miss Ryan. "And it was the only statue of his he ever signed."

"It's better than any of the pictures of it!" said Judith. "The expression on His Mother's face is so moving."

"*Pieta* means pity," said Miss Ryan. "This work is certainly the personification of it."

They walked slowly along the great Basilica with Miss Ryan pointing out the highlights to them until they reached the bronze statue of St Peter enthroned. The right foot of this statue had been worn smooth by centuries of kissing by the faithful. It took some time for the girls to get near to it as the modern faithful in their hundreds seemed more interested in being photographed with it rather than just kissing it.

They hadn't time to see any more then, as it was coming near to audience with the Pope time.

Miss Ryan hurried them out, promising to come back later on for another session.

The papal audience was held in Paul VI hall, an enormous room packed with people. St Brigid's were seated in a fairly good place, quite near to the front of the hall where there was a stage with rows of chairs on it. Quite a few bishops and cardinals were already seated there. Then a priest came out and announced in four different languages what the procedure would be and what he wanted the people to do. To the relief of many, English was one of the languages he spoke in.

About twenty minutes later they heard the sound of music and everyone in the hall rose to their feet. Most people turned around, craning to see what was happening, dozens even jumped on to their chairs to see better. The sound of clicking cameras came from all sides.

Nuala and Aileen, who were at the end of the row nearest to the central aisle, could see a group of people moving slowly up it, stopping now and again. "The one in white is the Pope," hissed Aileen excitedly.

"As if I needed to be told that!" Nuala said indignantly to her mother afterwards when she was describing the audience to her.

Mrs O'Donnell laughed. "Excitement makes people say funny things, what happened next?"

"The Pope eventually reached the stage, then he sat down in the middle of the front row as you can imagine. Everyone was clapping and cheering and the priest at the microphone had to ask us all to keep quiet," said Nuala. "Then a few people read the lesson and Gospel of the day in several different languages, including English, which took quite a lot of time."

"What were the other languages?" asked her mother.

"Italian, French and German. Then the Pope gave a homily in Italian which wasn't translated. Apparently if you are really keen, it's published the next day in English in the Vatican newspaper."

"I take it none of you were that keen," said her mother.

"Need you ask!" grinned Nuala. "Anyway, then every group in the hall was called out by name. When St Brigid's was called, we did like everyone else and got up and cheered. There were some other groups from Ireland who were waving little flags all the time. Some people sang for the Pope. I felt sorry for him, imagine every week he has to sit through an hour of groups from all over the world singing more or less the same holy songs."

"Were there people from all over the world there?" asked Mrs O'Donnell.

"Definitely! And not all of them were even Catholic. Near us were some Lutherans from Sweden. Anyway the whole thing ended with the Pope saying the "Our Father" in Latin with the whole lot of us."

"You don't know the "Our Father" in Latin, do you?"

"Of course we do. Sr Gobnait had us all

coached before we left St B's." said Nuala. "But then the Pope started walking down the centre aisle again on his way out and, you won't believe this, some of the fifth years managed to get close enough to have themselves photographed with him. Weren't we jealous!"

"Not the fifth years in your hotel?" asked Mrs O'Donnell.

"Yes, Sharon Kennedy and Lisa Shevlin were two of them, that pair of all people! We were mad!"

The post office was the next place on their agenda, once they had left the audience hall. Strangely enough, it seemed that everyone else had the same idea. "Miss Grimes was right," said Josie. "Much as I hate to admit it. The postcards are much cheaper here and the selection is brilliant."

"That must be the reason why it's so packed," panted Judith. "I was nearly squeezed to death in there but the girls were very efficient and pleasant."

"There were plenty of them, too," said Josie.

Nuala and Aileen weren't as fortunate as their friends in getting out of the post office, their queue having being held up by one man who seemed to have a lot of queries about the post. However, they eventually got their turn at the counter. It was then the work of a moment to put on the stamps.

"Now that the most important work of the day

is done," said Aileen, dropping her bundle of cards into the box marked airmail, "what do we do now?"

"We have to meet at the obelisk in the *piazza* first, then I think it's feeding time," said Nuala lightly, as she dropped her mail into the box too.

When they emerged out of the shop there was no sign of Miss Ryan or the rest of their group. "They must have gone ahead to the obelisk," said Aileen. "It was a good idea of Miss Ryan's to have that as a meeting place, it gives us a bit of freedom."

"It certainly would be hard to miss it," said Nuala. "It's so tall. Anyway, we'll go through the famous columns into the *piazza*. If we've time I would like to stand on the round stone between the fountain and the obelisk and see if it's true that when you look at the columns from it, it looks like one row instead of four rows."

"What do you mean – 'if it's true' – it must be true or someone would have said it before now," said Aileen.

Nuala shook her head in mock reproof. "You'll never make a scientist with that attitude," she said. "Scientists query everything that's said, unless they make the statement themselves, of course."

"I'm not going to be a scientist, anyway," said Aileen. "I rather fancy myself as a journalist, travelling the world reporting on hot spots and having interviews with famous people."

"No, no," said Nuala. "That's more Eithne's

line. You I see as something more glamorous for instance, er . . . "

Aileen was not destined to hear what her glamorous future was, for at that moment a thin sallow-faced woman stepped out from behind the enormous column they were passing, effectively barring their way. "Scusi," she said. "Remember me, we met in St Paul's."

Nuala and Aileen stared at the woman for a moment. "The negative woman," gasped Nuala. "I had forgotten all about you and the negatives."

"So had I," said Aileen. "We were having too good a time to think of them."

"You have them still?" asked the woman eagerly.

"I have," said Nuala. "Do you still want them?"

"*Si, si.* I will buy them from you. A hundred dollars, that would buy some nice things for young girls like you."

"I don't want to sell them," said Nuala. "But if you would tell me why you wanted them I might change my mind."

"It's to prevent a great wrong being done to someone," the woman said quickly. "A very great wrong."

"That doesn't tell me much," said Nuala. "I would need some more information than that."

"Well," said the woman. "I will tell you the whole story. My poor mother, who lives in *Firenze*, desperately needs an operation to save her life. It will cost a fortune, we have saved as much as we can, but alas we need so much more and time is running out for her. Now these negatives belong to a famous person, who asked me to find them for her, they were lost a few weeks ago. If I bring them back to her, she will give me enough money to cover the hospital costs." She wiped a tear from her eye as she spoke.

Nuala didn't know what to do, or even think. She looked across the *piazza* at the crowds of devout pilgrims walking towards St Peter's. She felt torn in two, maybe the woman was telling the truth, though she had her suspicions. "There was a man looking for them, is he a friend of yours?" she asked.

"No, he is a reporter, I think," the woman said quickly. "He probably wants the negatives to make a scandal, in fact, perhaps he was the one who stole them in the beginning."

Nuala decided to take a chance although her instinct told her otherwise. "Maybe I should go to the police with them," she said, as she fumbled with her belt.

"It wouldn't do any good," the woman said quickly. "If I told you the name of the famous person, you would understand." She looked around fearfully. Then to their surprise she said in a quick low voice, "I have to go. I will contact you later."

She seemed to melt behind the huge column again. Nuala and Aileen looked around them. The only person they could see near to them was a nun walking rapidly towards the Basilica, not an unusual sight in the Vatican. "What a weird encounter," said Nuala as they walked across to the obelisk. "What do you think, Aileen?"

"I don't believe she has a mother or that there is a place called *Firenze*, and I've just remembered that Josie told us that she saw her driving away from St Paul's with that guy in a car," said Aileen.

"You're right, what an idiot I am," said Nuala. "I was nearly taken in by her too, though *Firenze* is only Florence and she could have a mother there for all we know."

"I would have to have proof before I'd believe anything that one would say," said Aileen. "You see, Nuala, I am training to be the scientific type."

Miss Ryan, normally so good-tempered, was quite annoyed when Nuala and Aileen finally arrived at the meeting place. "What kept you girls?" she said crossly. "We must be standing waiting here for at least twenty minutes. Everyone is hungry and we have yet to visit the Sistine Chapel, not to mention several other places."

"I'm really very sorry, Miss Ryan," said Nuala apologetically. She was about to launch into a description of the woman who had stopped them, when fortunately she realised the complications that would ensue if she did.

"It wasn't really our fault," said Aileen. We were kept for ages in the post office."

"Very well, but don't let it happen again," said the teacher as she led them across to look for something to eat.

Later as they were sitting on stone seats at the the corner of the *Via della Conciliazione*, facing St

Peter's, Nuala and Aileen told Judith and Josie about their encounter between Bernini's columns. "That's the latest update on the negatives," said Nuala, breaking off a piece of her roll and giving it to a group of friendly pigeons who had come over for a bite. "I don't know what to do really, I suppose I'll have to wait and see what happens next."

"It's very exciting," said Josie. "I wonder what frightened her off?"

"Don't trust her, Nuala," said Judith. "If she was genuine she wouldn't have run away like that."

Miss Ryan came out of the restaurant behind them, with the rest of the girls. "Nuala," she said. "Don't you realise that St Peter's Square is full of people eating and the only place the pigeons are congregating for scraps is around you? Look for yourself."

"We had a sweet little dog here a minute ago," said Judith. "He reminded me of Chips, my dog at home."

Nuala looked around her, it was true: none of the pigeons were pecking around the crowds buying from the mobile vans dispensing, among other foods, pizzas, sandwiches, ice cream and drink.

"See that sole white pigeon among all the grey pigeons, Miss Ryan," she said. "It's really an angel in disguise, he's the one telling them to go over here. 'Pigeons of St Peter's,' I heard him say, 'that's Nuala from St Brigid's on the Boyne, she's very kind and will share your food with you.'"

156

17

Pieces of Paper

It was quite a subdued group who walked slowly back to St Peter's from their visit to the Vatican museums and the Sistine Chapel.

"It's hard to describe how I feel, sort of stuffed, I suppose," said Josie. "Several hours of art treasures and museums is a bit like eating too much rich food at one go."

"You certainly have your own way of describing things," said Miss Ryan in an amused voice. "But you're right, Josie. I have the same feeling."

"Judith is in a trance," said Aileen. "The Sistine Chapel really got to her. I preferred the *Raphael Stanze* myself."

"Hark the art expert," said Josie jeeringly. "I bet you can't remember one painting in them."

"Is that so, Miss Cleary! I bet you can't even remember the one I liked best. It's the one where St Peter, tied up in chains, is lying asleep and an angel is bending over him. The whole picture is lit up by the light coming from the angel. It's brilliant!"

"I loved that one too. You look through prison

bars at it. The light is fabulous, really strong from the angel and then softening out as it lights up the room," said Nuala. "I can't remember its name, though."

"*The Liberation* or *Delivery of St Peter*," said Miss Ryan. "It's considered one of Raphael's masterpieces."

"I'm not surprised. I told you it was brilliant," said Aileen complacently.

"There were so many rooms we had to go through," said Eithne. "Remember the room just full of maps and the next one was full of tapestries, designed by famous artists."

"What did you like best, Miss Ryan?" asked Monica. "I thought the *Last Judgement* in the Sistine Chapel was really scary."

"It's hard to say," replied the teacher. "The Sistine Chapel was breathtaking, as were the *Raphael Stanze*, but there were other paintings that appealed to me too. I agree about the *Last Judgement* though, Monica. I think Michelangelo meant it to be scary."

"It's a pity we have to see everything at one go," said Judith. "It must be great to be able to come back several times and spend hours at each place."

"You'll just have to win the Lottery, Judith," said the teacher. "Then you could spend months in Rome seeing it your way."

"You'd need to win the Lottery to spend months here," said Fidelma. "Where are we going now, Miss Ryan?"

"I think we should have a snack," she said, looking at her watch. "We have to go back to St Peter's and pick up from where we left off. I'll do that quickly so that we can go up in the lift to the top of the dome. It would be a shame to miss that experience and view over Rome."

"That sounds great," said Gwendoline. "Do you think we'd have time to go in and look for some religious present for my grandmother?"

"That's no problem, we'll do it now, then we can buy something to eat at one of those vans outside the shops opposite St Peter's Square," said Miss Ryan pleasantly. "Nuala's friends will be pleased to see her again, I dare say."

Nuala smiled absently. Even though she, like the rest of her friends, had been fascinated by the Sistine Chapel and the Vatican museums, she hadn't forgotten Giulia. Their encounter with her at the Bernini columns nagged away at her mind. Now as they were walking back to St Peter's, she wondered for the hundredth time could the woman have been telling them the truth? The fact that Josie had seen her in a car with the sad-eyed singer was a point against her, she knew. Then she remembered the tears in her eyes when she spoke about her mother in *Firenze*. Looking around at the cheerful pilgrims chatting and laughing in the sun, the sight of the huge Basilica ahead of her and the almost tangible religious feeling in the air, Nuala began to think that she was being a bit too hard on the unfortunate woman.

She had reached the point where she was

about to tell Aileen that she had decided to hand over the negatives to the woman if she turned up again. After all, they had never been theirs in the first place, anyway. She looked for Aileen and was surprised to see that everyone was clustered around a newsstand at the post office, just ahead of her. As she hurried to catch up she could hear Josie say, "Look, everyone, they sell English newspapers here!"

Then she saw Aileen turn around and heard her call, "Nuala, where's Nuala, she must read this!"

"What must I read?" said Nuala, looking over her shoulder. Then she saw the headline *Roman police still baffled by photographic break-in*. Grabbing the paper she read:

```
In Rome today senior police officers
confirmed that they have no lead yet into
the mysterious break-in two weeks ago at
Pentic Studios when photographic negatives
waiting to be collected were stolen. Police
spokesperson, Alvaro Carmela, fears that
blackmail may have been the motive behind
this robbery, as all the negatives taken
had been the property of an investigative
team, working for the European Union.
```

Nuala dropped the newspaper limply back on the stand. "Aileen," she said. "They're blackmailers and I nearly gave the negatives to her. Well, that's that, I'll destroy them the minute I get back to the hotel."

"Why don't you go to the police?" asked Judith.

Nuala thought for a minute. "No, it would only cause trouble all round, remember we found them in that suede jacket. If I destroy them, nobody will be hurt. It's the best way, especially as we go home tomorrow."

"Come along, girls," called Miss Ryan. "Don't be wasting time. If we don't hurry, we'll miss our chance of going up to the dome." At the same time as the girls were moving away from the newspapers outside the post office, on the other side of Rome the Contessa was speaking to her friend in Brussels.

"I have a plan," she was saying, "which I am confident will produce those negatives. In fact, by this time tomorrow they will be destroyed and we will be safe. I will contact you by 14:00 hours without fail."

"Good, otherwise I will have no option but to resign and disappear from public life. I must go now. I'm very busy with meetings for the rest of the day. *Arrivederci*."

"*Arrivederci*," said the Contessa, putting down the phone.

Miss Ryan led the third years to a shop so that Gwendoline could buy a present for her granny. It not only sold gifts of every kind, but was also a *bureau de change*, which suited Miss Ryan too. So while she and Gwendoline got on with their business, the rest of the girls wandered around, looking at the goods, some of which were very expensive. The Murrays, tiring of this dull stuff, slipped out to investigate the nearby food vans. They came back quickly with the information that while all the van prices were exorbitant, the one on the left-hand side of the square was a good bit cheaper than the one on the right-hand side.

Armed with this knowledge they all went to the left-hand one, where they bought slices of pizza, cakes or ice cream according to their tastes, washed down by chilled orange or lemon squash, a poor substitute for *Jungle* was the opinion of all.

Then it was once again mingling with the crowds into St Peter's for their final visit. They had a quick look at St Pius X, whose incorrupt body lies in a big glass casket in one of the side chapels of the Basilica.

As they walked back down the central aisle at the end of the visit, Miss Ryan pointed out the statues of all the saints who were also founders of religious orders which line it on either side. It was quite interesting to see Saints Ignatius, Vincent de Paul, Dominic etc.

"They are all men," said Josie. "I don't see any women saints among them."

"Let's check," said Aileen. So they went up and down carefully checking each saintly statue, finding that two women had made the front line, St Theresa of Avila and St Madeline Sophie Barat.

"I suppose two is better than nothing," said Josie.

"There are plenty of women saints on plaques on the walls," said Miss Ryan. "I suppose they had used up all the centre aisle, before these were even canonised."

"I suppose so," Josie conceded. "But I am not pleased at this discrimination."

Miss Ryan laughed. "Well Josie, nothing's stopping you from becoming a holy founder and swelling the ranks of women in St Peter's." A haughty sniff was all Miss Ryan got in reply for this remark.

Then they said goodbye to St Peter's, walking down the steps and turning to the left on their way to the entrance to the dome. "I'm really looking forward to this," said Miss Ryan. "I've been told that when you walk out on the roof of St Peter's, the sensation is like walking on the deck of a ship, with only the blue sky above you, and also that the view over Rome is stupendous."

"It sounds brilliant," said Gwendoline. "I must take plenty of photos there."

"Are we going all the way up to the very top?" asked Eithne.

"No, the lift only goes up to the roof," said the teacher. "I believe the last stairs up to the very top are very steep and narrow, with only a rope to hang on to as you climb."

"Where are Aileen and Nuala?" asked Josie, looking behind them. "I didn't see them come out of St Peter's with us."

"They did," said Judith. "Don't worry, they know where to go; they'll catch up in a minute."

As Nuala and Aileen walked out of the Basilica, a crowd of people came walking along behind them, passing them out and effectively cutting them off from the rest of their party. In consequence they felt free to discuss that burning topic, the newspaper report about the theft of the negatives.

"Wouldn't you love to know the significance of those negatives to this investigating team," said Nuala.

"I thought you said that they were industrial spies," said Aileen, puzzled at Nuala's remark.

"They could still be spies, though that newspaper report puts a different complexion on things, as it mentions blackmail," said Nuala. "Of course, spies can be blackmailed too. Either way, that pair are crooks."

"I never believed all that guff about her mother's operation," said Aileen. "Though I felt you did."

"It's this place, it has a peculiar effect on me," said Nuala. "But don't worry, the softie mood has passed. I wouldn't give that one anything now."

They were so engrossed in their conversation that neither of them noticed a familiar figure falling into step beside them, as the people in front were quite noisy. "Hand over the negatives," said a quiet voice beside Nuala, making her jump, when she felt something hard pressed against her side. "I gave you a chance of selling them to me, now you'll have it the hard way."

"Certainly not," said Nuala. "We've read that newspaper report and we know what your game is now."

The woman looked puzzled, then she replied in an annoyed voice. "What game, there is no game here. I told you the truth, but I'm in a hurry so hand them over or else."

Nuala was terrified, then she remembered the strict security they had at St Peter's, everyone was scrutinised as they passed in and out. The woman must be bluffing. "I'll never give those negatives to you," she said. "Come on, Aileen, run!"

She dashed off, with Aileen close behind her quickly catching up with the rest of the group as they passed into the entrance to the dome.

They were just in time to catch the lift. As soon as they were all in and it had started off, Nuala asked, "Anyone got a scissors?" and she took the negatives out of her money belt.

Fortunately Judith had a tiny nail scissors with her so Nuala quickly chopped the five negatives into tiny pieces finishing just as they arrived at the roof. "There's the singing guy out there on the roof," warned Judith.

Nuala turned and started climbing the steep staircase which led to the top of the dome. She pulled herself up the rope, a precarious undertaking in the circumstances as her left hand was full of tiny pieces of film.

Panting, she reached the top. Moving swiftly around the balcony there, she found a convenient aperture and scattered the negatives to the four winds through it. "Now," she said triumphantly. "No one will ever be blackmailed by those negatives again."

She turned in time to see the sad-eyed singer leave the balcony and slip out of sight, presumably to tell the news to his partner.

18

Funny Fioretti

A concerned Aileen and Judith joined Nuala a few minutes later with strict instructions from Miss Ryan that they weren't to delay but to bring her back down to the roof where the others were, as quickly as possible. Great was their rejoicing when Nuala told them what she had done and how her action had been observed by the sad-eyed singer.

"That's foiled them, anyway," said Aileen with satisfaction. "Maybe that will get them out of our hair now."

"Let's take a quick look out at Rome spread in front of us," said Judith, "now that we're here."

"Wow," said Aileen leaning over the balcony and gazing at St Peter's Square and the long straight street leading for miles off it, clustered with buildings and sidestreets far below them all looking as small as doll's houses.

"We must be really high up here, just look at the obelisk in St Peter's Square, it's tiny!"

"Even those huge statues on the roof of the Basilica look small from here," said Judith.

"Do you see that red dot about the size of the head of a pin, there on the corner of the big street, opposite the obelisk?" said Aileen. "Well, that's the van we bought our snacks from."

"The view is fantastic," agreed Nuala. "But I don't really care any more, I just want to go back to the hotel, I feel so tired."

"It's the reaction setting in," said Judith. "After the excitement of foiling the blackmailers."

"Come on," said Aileen, looking worried. "We'd better get back to Miss Ryan, she'll be mad if we delay too much."

Coincidently, Enrico and Giulia at that moment were passing the very red van which Aileen had pointed out to her friends from the dome. "Why didn't you use your gun?" Enrico said, breaking the heavy silence which lay between them.

"I did, but she just ran away," Giulia said shortly. "I was taken by surprise. You didn't expect me to fire the gun just beside the Basilica, in the middle of all those people, did you? I would have been in big trouble then."

"What do we do now?" he asked.

"Get out of Rome fast," was her terse reply. "That Contessa is a tough woman with powerful friends. I was sure I saw her here today. I'm quitting before she comes after me for that 10,000 dollars I got from her."

"Where could I go?" he asked, looking sadder than ever.

"Come with me to *Firenze*," said Giuila, looking kindly at him. "There's always plenty of tourists there. You could sing your Mario Lanza songs to them, couldn't you?"

His sad eyes lit up. "Your mother wouldn't mind?" he asked.

Giuila laughed. "Not her. If you're coming, let's go, my car is around the corner."

"What about Roberto?" he asked.

"Forget him, he stole the negatives from Pentic in the beginning. I know too much about him. He won't bother us."

"In that case, I'll go with you." They walked off arm in arm, Enrico humming happily: *"Once you have found her never let her go."*

The Angelus was ringing when the girls from St Brigid's assembled in St Peter's Square to set off to board the coach for their return journey. Aileen and Judith, waiting for Nuala, were stunned to see her in close conversation with the dreaded Sharon and Lisa, who seemed to be doing all the talking. However, when Nuala ran over to them, she didn't seem distressed at all.

"What did that pair want?" snapped Aileen suspiciously.

Nuala laughed. "They're cracked," she said. "They went on saying it was only a joke and they didn't mean it and would I ever forgive them."

"It must have been something the Pope said to them," said Judith. "All that forgiveness stuff sounds like him."

Aileen would have none of that chat. "What were they talking about?" she demanded impatiently.

"I don't know really, something about a nasty letter," said Nuala. "I just said 'of course, that's all right' and fled, it was so embarrassing!"

"A letter," said Aileen. "The only letter you got was from the crooks, I don't remember another one."

Nuala stared at them, then she started to laugh. "What a scream, the letter that worried me so much wasn't from the blackmailers at all, it was from Lisa and Sharon. How funny. I wonder why they sent it."

"All that 'beware' stuff and 'we'll be watching you' was from them," said Aileen. "I can't believe it!"

Josie appeared beside them. "Did you hear that Eithne and Fidelma frightened the fifth years so much the other night that they walked straight into Miss Grimes!" she said excitedly. "They were nipping out to have a bit of crack in the Irish Bar around the corner! But don't talk about it as they're afraid the fifth years will take a hideous revenge on them if they ever find out that it was them who played the trick."

"Tell them not to worry," said Nuala. "The fifth years thought that it was me and I've forgiven them."

Judith and Aileen looked at Nuala, then they burst out laughing. "What's the joke?" asked Josie, looking very puzzled.

"Sit beside me in the coach," said Aileen kindly. "I'll explain it all to you."

Later that evening Nuala produced a square

package, handing it to Miss Ryan. "It's just a little present to express our thanks," she said. "It's from all of us third years."

"You really made this Roman tour for us," said Judith.

"It was brilliant," said Josie. "I'm sure we had the best time of all."

Miss Ryan was delighted with her earrings, which were a pair of crescent moons in silver. "They're beautiful," she said, trying them on. "Thank you very much. I really enjoyed the tour too."

Everyone was up bright and early on the following morning doing their packing and any last-minute shopping. Now that the final day had arrived there was an air of excited expectancy among the girls. "I'm looking forward to getting home again," said Monica. "We'll have loads to tell our families, won't we?"

"So am I," said Gwendoline, "and handing out our presents too. I'm sure your mum will love the handbag."

"I hope so. I'm all packed," said Monica. "Will we take our bags down to the desk now?"

As they staggered out of the lift with their luggage, they could see a worried-looking Miss Ryan standing beside a pile of cases and bags, talking to Nuala and Aileen.

"As Signora Fioretti has sent her car for you, I suppose it would be rude not to accept her invitation," the teacher was saying as they came up and dumped their cases beside the other ones on the floor. "The only trouble is the coach will be here at 1 p.m. to take us to the airport."

"It's only 11 a.m. now," said Nuala. "We should be back in loads of time for the coach."

"I think I'll go and discuss it with Miss Grimes," said the teacher. "Have you everything packed?"

"Yes, Miss Ryan," said Aileen. "Judith and Josie are on their way down with their cases too."

When the teacher had left Monica and Gwendoline plied Nuala and Aileen with questions. "Where are you going?" they asked.

"Signora Fioretti has invited Nuala, Judith, Josie and myself to visit her this morning," explained Aileen. "She sent a car to take us to her villa."

"Wow, you lucky things," said Monica. "I wish she had invited me."

"Me too," said Gwendoline. "Where does she live?"

"Somewhere in Rome, I suppose," said Nuala.

Miss Ryan came back with Josie and Judith. "Now, girls," she said briskly. "Miss Grimes suggests that I take you to see the Signora. I'll take our tickets. Leave everything ready in case we're delayed, so that all we will have to do when we return is get into the coach, not that I anticipate any such problem."

Five minutes later an awed Monica and Gwendoline watched enviously as the four friends and their teacher were whisked away from the hotel in a gleaming white Lamborghini car. The traffic, as always, was fast and furious. Nobody

171

spoke in the car as it sped through the streets eventually coming to a stop outside some high metal doors, very similar to the one they had once seen open. As soon as the car stopped, the big doors opened and the car slid quietly through them, stopping in front of a tall house there.

They got out of the car feeling quite intimidated by the opulence around them. "It's very like the one we saw that night," whispered Aileen. "There's even a fountain in the middle of the courtyard."

"It is," whispered Nuala back to her. "Gwendoline must have been right about the Fioretti wealth, after all."

The driver of the car led them to the front door of the house, which was opened immediately by a woman dressed in black. She took them to a salon, politely requesting them to enter and wait for the *signora*. Then she left the room, closing the door behind her.

The five walked across the room, their footsteps echoing on the marble floor. A long narrow French door opened and a woman came in and stood looking at them, a pleased expression on her face. "Welcome to my humble abode, girls of St Brigid's," she said in a mocking voice.

The four girls stared at the women in utter disbelief, then Nuala found her tongue. "What are *you* doing here?" she asked. "Sister Mercy, or whatever you call yourself now."

"Nuala O'Donnell giving trouble as usual! With all the cities in the world to pick, why did you have to come to Rome and interfere in our business?"

19

Arrivederci Roma

A very puzzled Miss Ryan looked first at Nuala, then at the woman and back at Nuala again. "Isn't this Signora Fioretti, then?" she asked. "The one who invited us to her house?"

"No, she isn't," said Nuala. "She tricked us into coming here by pretending to be Miss Keane, or rather Signora Fioretti, and I think I know why too."

"What's going on?" asked the unfortunate teacher. "Who is she then?"

"I can't tell you what her real name is but surely you've heard about the Borgia and Mercy scandal at St Brigid's. She's Mercy."

Miss Ryan looked stunned and apprehensive, obviously she had heard the whole story.

That's enough from you," said the woman. "I am *la Contessa* and this is my home. Now that you're here, hand over those negatives at once. Don't bother pretending that you don't know what I'm talking about either. I know you have them."

"I know all about those negatives, but as it happens I haven't got them with me. In fact, they

173

are in a safe place, a very safe place," said Nuala, seeing her in mind's eye all the tiny bits of the negatives floating away on the breeze above St Peter's.

"That's no problem, you can send for them. I know you're going back to Ireland today and that your plane is due to leave Rome at 15:00 hours. I've no intention of letting you get on that plane as long as you are in possession of those negatives!" said the Contessa nastily, noticing with satisfaction the anxious looks on their faces.

"You can't keep us here!" said Miss Ryan indignantly.

"Can't I just! Sit down," she ordered, taking a gun out of her pocket with a casual air and placing it on the plush velvet cloth which covered an occasional table beside her.

They immediately obeyed. Four of them perched themselves uncomfortably on the edge of an elegant chaise-longue, the fifth, Judith, on a nearby armchair. Nuala tried desperately to think of some way of circumventing the Contessa, particularly as she remembered how roughly she had treated Judith and herself in a previous confrontation.

"If I tell you where the negatives are, will you let us go?" she said, catching sight of the time on an ornate wall clock.

"It depends," said the Contessa. "As long as you come with me, of course."

Judith, sitting on her armchair, slightly away from the chaise-longue, was thinking too. Like

Nuala, she passionately desired to get the better of the Contessa. The heavily-embossed velvet tablecloth caught her eye, bringing memories of the time when she and Nuala had been kidnapped.

"The negatives are hidden in St Peter's Basilica," said Nuala, with a great air of candour. The Contessa looked annoyed.

"Where in the Basilica?" she asked shortly.

"In the dome itself," said Nuala promptly.

"I don't believe a word of it," snapped the Contessa. She picked up her gun and walked over to Nuala and stood threateningly over her. "Don't play games with me. You'll regret it!" she said through clenched teeth.

Judith saw her chance. Tiptoeing swiftly across to the table, she snatched the heavy velvet cloth from it, throwing it over the unsuspecting Contessa. "Help! Miss Ryan," called Judith. "Help!" The Contessa fought like a wildcat, but the combined effect of the girls and teacher was too much for her. The Contessa dropped her gun and five minutes later she was trussed up in the velvet cloth like a rolled-up carpet.

"Quick girls, let's go," said Miss Ryan, rushing out of the room. The girls swiftly followed her. Josie, the last one out, slammed the door shut behind her, causing the heavy framed picture of the Contessa's grandfather to fall off the wall. His hapless granddaughter, emerging from the velvet cloth, received the full brunt of it. She gave a grunt, slipping unconscious to the floor.

Outside in the peaceful courtyard the fountains played as usual in the sun. "Walk quickly but don't panic and run," Miss Ryan whispered to them. "There doesn't seem to be anyone around, thank goodness."

"It's the siesta hour," said Judith. "But how will we get those huge doors open?"

As they walked along, keen-eyed Aileen spotted a little door leading out of a back wall. Soon they were running down an empty street, which as luck would have it led them straight out on the street familiar to them. It was the *Via Merulana*. Miss Ryan looked at her watch. "Gosh, how the time has flown!" she groaned. "We'll never make the airport in time. We'll go to the hotel anyway and get a taxi there."

Panting with the heat, they walked as fast as possible towards the hotel. Just as Judith felt she couldn't go on for much longer, a car drew up quite close and somebody hailed them. "Don't pay any attention, girls. Really, these Italian men!" said Miss Ryan, marching on.

They could hear the car starting and drive slowly on, passing them out. Then it stopped again and this time a man jumped out, calling, "Vanessa, Vanessa, it's me, Felix!"

Miss Ryan stopped and stared, then she rushed over clutching his arm. "Felix, could you drive us to the airport, our plane leaves at three!"

Somehow or other the exhausted teacher and girls squashed into the back of the taxi. Felix jumped in beside the driver, speaking to him in Italian. The driver turned the car and went speeding off across Rome, presumably in the direction of the airport.

Vanessa explained as well as she could to Felix what had happened, even though the whole event had been a complete mystery to her. On arrival at the airport, they only had time to thank Felix before running in search of their particular airline desk. Vanessa lingered a minute longer, thanking him again.

"Don't mention it. It's always fun to rescue a fair maiden," he said, laughing. "But few of us get a chance to rescue five in one go. I'll ring you in Dublin next week, I hope to hear the rest of the story then."

"I hope I'll know the whole of it myself by then," she said. "Goodbye and thanks again."

When they explained their problem to the Italian at the desk, he was most upset. "I think your plane is about to go," he said, then he started speaking in rapid Italian on his mobile phone. "Come with me," he said, charging on to another desk where, to the surprise of the anxious girls, he started talking in rapid Italian again. After doing this twice more, he announced, "Your seats have been sold, but you're lucky, they will give you seats in club class." He sounded surprised.

"Club class? What's that?" asked Aileen in a low voice.

"It's between tourist class and first class," said the more experienced Judith.

177

"Whoopee," said Josie. "Won't the others just be green with envy!"

In no time at all they were being escorted over the tarmac, where the plane was waiting to receive them before taking off. "Welcome on board," said the smiling flight attendants.

"I think the biggest difference between the classes must be the amount of room," said Nuala as they fastened their seat belts. "There's loads more in here. I must say it's very comfortable. I shall always travel club class, it suits my temperament."

"Me too," said Aileen. "Wasn't Judith brilliant back there, nobbling Mercy with the tablecloth?"

"She was, it reminded me of the time we did likewise with Miss Smith in the car."

"We're moving," said Aileen, looking out the window of the plane. "Wow, we're rising fast. Goodbye Italy, goodbye Rome!"

Nuala grinned. "You mean *Arrivederci Roma*," she said. "I wonder what happened to our sad-eyed singer."

At about the same time as the plane was taking off from the airport, Roberto was entering the Contessa's salon. "This is not the time to be doing floor exercises," he said impatiently as he caught sight of her gyrating around on the velvet cloth.

"Do you realise that none of my staff turned up today. What am I to do?"

"Come fly with me, Roberto," she replied rising

up from the floor with a foolish smile on her face. "Come fly with me to the dome of St Peter's and there we shall find something, I can't remember what, which will save our dear Desirée from being stripped of her royal envoyship."

"Contessa, I'm shocked! I never knew before you were a secret drinker," he said rushing out of the room calling, "Bella, Bella!"

Meanwhile, back in the plane, a certain lassitude had fallen on Miss Ryan and her four pupils. A busy exciting morning foiling an old enemy followed by club class treatment had taken its toll.

"It has just struck me, Aileen, that in the last few days you haven't mentioned the crossword once," said Nuala, feeling a bit guilty. "Did you get it finished?"

"I nearly did, I've only two clues left, but I can't get them," said Aileen. "Pity, I would have have liked to have won a prize."

"If you had it here I could give you a hand," said Nuala lazily, "but I suppose it's in your case."

Aileen fished around in a little shoulder bag, producing a crumpled piece of paper. Spreading it out on the little tray in front of her, she said: "An aristocratic title originally meaning companion, eight letters? It has an O and a U in it. The other one is a Spanish family, six letters with an O and a G in it."

"Here, let me see," said Nuala. "The second one

179

is BORGIA! Well, what a pair of idiots we are. The other one could only be COUNTESS!"

Josie peered over their seat and hissed, "Miss Ryan says to order any free drink we like, so I ordered a small bottle of champagne for each of us!"

THE END (or finito).

ACROSS

6. Perfect soil for gardeners, (4)
*8. Large wolf like breed of dog,
   also called German Shepherd,(8)
9. Range of savage mood? (5)
10. They <u>were</u> - in the present,(3)
*11. A large stretch of water, (5)

12. Dig in the past, (3)
14. A French man, (5)

*16. Capital city of the state of
   Arizona, (7)
*20. Aristocratic title which
   originally meant companion,(8)
23. One of the seven deadly ..,(3)
*24. Affecting an oily charm (8)
25. Don't stop at green (2)
27. St Brigid was one of the
   many ..(6)
30. I love Latin (3)
31. Many of these in each street(6)
*32. Food flavouring made from
   the volatile oil of the
   climbing orchid (7)
33. Juice of the trees (3)

* = Clues which are
   given and solved in
   the book

DOWN

1. A Higher Angel (6)
*2. Capital of Sicily (7)
3. Something taken to be
   true without proof (6)
4. to to? (4)
*5. Decorative delicate
   fabric woven in an
   open web (4)
7. The lesson to be
   learnt from a
   story (5)
9. Join two words (3)
13. Aromatic forked root
   from China/N.America
   used medicinally(7)
*15. God of War(4)
*17. Legendary Greek King
   and hero of a work by
   Homer (8)
18. The Radiologist's
   machine (4)
*19. Spanish family (6)
21. You won't get one with
   sun block (3)
22. What elephants play in
   a mini (6)
24. Keats' Ode to a
   Grecian ...? (3)
26. To clean or an
   entertainment (4)
28. Another name for
   tavern (3)
29. ... Volatile? (3)
30. A silly donkey (3)

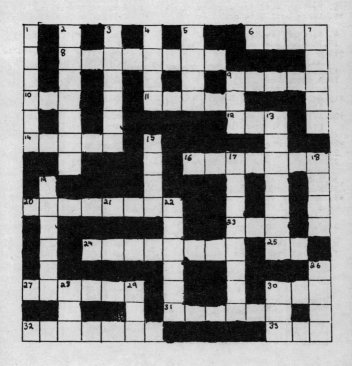